The

Science Fiction Series

Perfection Learning®

Jacob Goldman was trapped in a nightmare...

"So you won't talk, eh?" the monster boomed, stepping toward Jake menacingly. "I'm taking you in for questioning."

"I'd rather you didn't," Jake said, stepping away nervously.

"Come along," the monster said.

"No!" Jake replied, his voice trembling.

Jake dodged and ran away. He could hear the monster's footsteps thundering behind him. Despite its size and bulk, the monster was fast. And its stride was much longer than Jake's. Jake knew that it could easily catch up with him.

About the Author

D. F. Rider is a full-time writer who lives in Portland, Oregon. Rider has been a teacher, editor, novelist, educational writer, playwright, theater director, set designer, pizza cook, waiter, visual artist, and horse breeder. Rider has lived in ten different states, London, and Mexico.

Acknowledgments

I wish to thank the young people who contributed their ideas to this book: Scheyere Ballosingh, Kelly Block, Juliet Brown, Tonya Henry, and Fuey Saetern.

—D. F. Rider

Other Titles by D. F. Rider in The Decryptors Science Fiction Series:

Sibyl's Kind
Calendar's Years
The Fractal Caverns
The Nano Menace
The Virtual Ghost
The Lost Planet

In Your Dreams

by D. F. Rider

Perfection Learning

© 2001, 1995 Perfection Learning Corporation
1000 North Second Avenue, Logan, Iowa 51546

3 4 5 6 7 PP 09 08 07 06 05

Table of Contents

The Monster 1

The Legend 11

Lucidity 25

Oneironaut 35

Is This Really a Dream? 47

Doubles 61

Flying Lessons 71

No Trespassing 81

The Important Words 97

The Dungeon 109

Afterword 119

1

The Monster

Something was stalking Jake Goldman.

It was early morning. The first streaks of daylight were stealing the stars from the clear, blue sky. Jake was walking barefoot on a dirt path that wound along the edge of a rapidly flowing creek. The creek ran through a gully surrounded by towering cedars. Jake had no idea where he was. But somehow his surroundings seemed familiar.

How can a place be strange and familiar at the same time? he wondered. *And how did I get here, anyway? I seem to remember something about a door. Like I came here through some special kind of door...*

Something was moving in the trees on the other side of the creek. Jake was sure he saw a shadow lurking there, moving along with him. Something large and dark. How long had he been aware of it? Seconds? Minutes?

In Your Dreams

He couldn't remember.

Jake stopped and stared into the cedars across the creek. There wasn't yet enough light for him to see very well. Anyway, that moving shape didn't seem to be there now. But he still felt uneasy.

Jake turned away from the creek and began to climb the steep slope of a hill.

I've got to get home, he thought. He felt sure that he would reach home by climbing this hill—although he didn't know why he thought so. But when he reached the hilltop, he could see no houses. All he found was an open, grassy area surrounded by trees.

Where am I? Jake wondered.

He looked back down the slope. He could see out across the countryside. Here and there, the landscape was dotted with the white walls and red roofs of houses and barns. There were some open pastures and small fields, but most of the view was of trees. A single, tall mountain loomed over the eastern horizon. A huge, dark cloud hid the mountaintop.

Jake lowered his eyes and peered down toward the creek again, into the dimness beneath the cedars. It was too shadowy to see much of anything there—if there *was* anything to see.

The Monster

Silly, Jake thought. *Just my imagination. Who'd be stalking me, anyway?*

But he decided to stay on the hilltop and in the open, just to be safe. He turned and looked westward. He could see a long break in the trees. He knew that it marked the passage of a wide river just a few miles away. He also knew the name of that river.

The Willamette, Jake realized. *Yes, I know this place after all. So why does it seem so strange?*

He looked toward the forest on the river's far bank. He shook his head. What kept nagging at his mind? Why did he keep thinking that something was missing?

Then memories flooded his mind—images of tall buildings and bridges.

Where's the city?

Jake's stomach sank.

Where's downtown Portland? he wondered. *It should be on the other side of the river. Buildings should be shining in the sunlight. And right here, I should be standing in my own neighborhood. Where did this forest come from? There's not supposed to be a creek near here either.*

He shivered a little from chilliness. *And what am I doing outside at this time of the morning, anyhow? This can't be real. This has to be a dream.*

Yes, that was it! It had to be! All this was nothing but an unusually vivid dream. For a moment, Jake felt relieved. If this was a dream, all he had to do was to wake up.

But it didn't feel like a dream. He ran his bare feet through the damp leaves on the ground. The leaves clung between his toes. The soles of his feet hurt when he stepped on sharp stones in the soil. No, all this seemed much too real to be a dream.

But what else can *it be?* he wondered.

Jake had been having a lot of nightmares lately. He'd learned a special trick to make nightmares vanish.

Guess it's time for my little "nightmare speech," he decided.

"My name is Jacob Goldman," he whispered, his eyes closed tightly. "I'm fifteen years old. I live in Portland, Oregon. I go to Monroe High School. I was bar mitzvahed at the Beth Israel Synagogue. My dad's name is Tom and my mom's name is Paula. *And nothing that's happening to me right now is real!*"

That usually did the trick. Jake opened his eyes, expecting his dream to be gone.

It wasn't. The open hilltop still lay before him. That could only mean one thing.

This isn't a dream at all! Jake decided

The Monster

with alarm. *This is real!*

The sky was growing brighter by the minute. Jake now saw two teenage boys coming across the open hilltop toward him. But they didn't seem to be walking.

What are they doing? he asked himself.

Then he realized. They were flying! Well, not so much flying as gliding along about a foot or two off the ground. The two were moving toward him at a very brisk speed. At last they stopped, about three or four feet in front of Jake. They hovered in the air a moment; then they gracefully floated to the ground.

The two boys were dressed in roughly woven wool outfits and leather boots. The taller of the two teenagers was black, with short hair and an athletic build. He looked awfully familiar.

Robert Webster? Jake wondered, noticing the black teenager's resemblance to a close friend.

The shorter of the two had straight dark hair and green eyes. He looked familiar too. The shorter one spoke.

"Come with us," he said.

Then Jake realized something.

My voice! Jake realized. *That kid's speaking in my own voice! And he even looks like me—enough to be my twin!*

"Who are you?" Jake asked the two teenagers.

"It's not safe to talk here," Jake's double replied. "Come on! Hurry!"

Then the two teenagers turned and began to fly across the hilltop, still staying close to the ground. They were moving too quickly for Jake to follow on foot.

"Wait a minute!" Jake shouted. "I can't fly!"

"Sure, you can!" his double called back, still moving away. "Listen, you've got to learn what you can and can't do here—and fast!"

"But what's the danger?" Jake asked.

"Look behind you!" his double answered.

Jake turned back toward the trees. A huge gray shape came stomping up the slope from the direction of the gully. Jake's heart pounded with fear at what he saw.

It was a monster—a hulking, man-shaped figure. It appeared to be roughly modeled out of clay. Its limbs were bulky but flexible. Its face was particularly horrible to look at, with ill-shaped mouth, nose, and hair. Its eye sockets were deep and dark, but Jake saw something glowing in them, like red-hot coals. The creature looked like an unfinished sculpture, not a man at all. But it was definitely alive—and moving with remarkable speed.

The Monster

When the creature reached the top of the hill, it looked back and forth at Jake and the two boys flying away.

"Get away from there!" Jake's double called back to him.

"But where can I go?" Jake answered.

"The door!" Jake's double cried. "Head for the door!"

Then Jake's double and his companion disappeared into the nearby trees.

The door? Jake wondered.

The monster was now lumbering straight toward him. Jake froze with fear. The monster peered at him with its glowing eyes. It towered over Jake by at least four feet.

The monster began to speak in a low voice which boomed and echoed, as if over a loudspeaker.

"Where were you on the night of the tenth?" the monster asked.

"I—I don't know," Jake sputtered. "What day of the week was that, exactly?"

"Just answer the question," the monster replied.

Jake was too frightened to think. He couldn't remember what month it was, much less what he had been doing on the night of the tenth.

"So you won't talk, eh?" the monster

boomed, stepping toward Jake menacingly. "I'm taking you in for questioning."

"I'd rather you didn't," Jake said, stepping away nervously.

"Come along," the monster said.

"No!" Jake replied, his voice trembling.

Jake dodged and ran away. He could hear the monster's footsteps thundering behind him. Despite its size and bulk, the monster was fast. And its stride was much longer than Jake's. Jake knew that it could easily catch up with him.

Then Jake saw something up ahead. It was a door! A plain, wooden door. It wasn't part of a house or a wall. It was just standing there by itself, framed between two trees. It didn't seem to lead anywhere. Even so, Jake dashed toward it.

This must be the door that kid mentioned, Jake thought.

Jake ran as fast as he could. He dug his bare feet into the earth. He gasped for breath. He drove himself faster and faster. But in his desperation to get away from the monster, he felt like he was slowing down, not speeding up. And he could hear the monster's thundering footsteps coming closer and closer.

Jake wished he would wake up. Wished he could sigh with relief to find that this

The Monster

whole experience was just a dream. But somehow he knew that it wasn't a dream. It was some sort of strange reality.

Desperately, Jake tried to increase his stride. He wished he could fly. But if his mad dash across the clearing hadn't made him airborne, nothing would.

Jake felt the monster's clay hands snatching at him, just barely missing his arms. In another split second, he knew the creature would catch him. The door loomed before him. He tumbled through it, quite certain that the monster would be upon him.

2

The Legend

Jake crouched down. He squeezed his eyes shut and braced for the monster's grip. But nothing happened. He noticed that the ground beneath him had changed. It was no longer grass and rough soil.

Floorboards, Jake realized.

Jake opened his eyes. The monster was gone. The gray light of early morning fell on familiar clothes piled on a chair. He was back in his own bedroom.

"So it *was* a dream!" he whispered aloud.

But that seemed impossible to believe. The whole experience had been too real. Still, what *else* could it have been?

Jake was still panting fearfully. He stood up slowly and looked around. He was on the

In Your Dreams

floor beside his bed.

Did I fall out of bed during my dream? he wondered.

He half expected the wood-paneled wall of his room to change into a forest. But everything was back to normal. He heard a car start outside his closed window. He rose to his feet and looked out the window. It was a gray January day in Portland, Oregon.

Jake felt tired—much as if he really had been running for his life. He briefly considered going back to bed. He didn't really have to get up for another fifteen minutes, judging by the clock. But he decided that he didn't want to go back to sleep. He didn't want to risk falling back into that nightmare. In fact, he didn't think he'd ever want to go to sleep again.

As Jake walked toward his closet, he realized that one foot was sore. He looked at it closely and gasped in astonishment. He had a small cut on his ankle. But that wasn't what startled him. His feet were muddy. He looked down at his rumpled pajamas. A leaf clung to one leg.

I've been walking in my sleep! he thought. *Now that's carrying a dream too far!*

Jake reached into his tiny closet for school clothes. His room had been designed as a

The Legend

small den or office space. With the bed and a desk in it, it wasn't exactly spacious. But he didn't have to share it with anyone, and Jake loved it for that reason.

Jake went into the living room just in time to see his mother and two sisters dashing around on their way out. His older sister, Deborah, went to the community college where his mother was an art teacher. Debby and his mother would take the family car and drop Jake's younger sister, Rosalie, off at her middle school. Jake's father was probably still asleep. He was the director of a theater group, and rehearsal had ended late the night before.

Jake gazed out the big front window of their townhouse apartment. On clear days he could see Mt. Hood's snowcapped peak. But today, as on most winter mornings, the mountain was hidden by a wall of gray mist.

Jake went into the kitchen. He found a clean frying pan and whipped up some scrambled eggs for himself and his grandmother. He put two plates piled with eggs and a couple of glasses of orange juice on the table. Just then, his grandmother walked into the kitchen.

"Good morning, Jake," his grandmother said brightly.

In Your Dreams

"Good morning, Bubbeh," Jake replied. *Bubbeh* is a Yiddish word for grandmother. He hadn't always called her Bubbeh. When he was younger, Jake had called her "Eileeo." That was his two-year-old's version of "Eileen," Bubbeh's real first name.

Bubbeh had never seemed very grandmotherly. True, her face showed all the usual wrinkles of a sixty-five-year-old. But her bright, cheerful expression was of someone much younger. So for most of his childhood, Jake had never thought of her as a grandmother at all.

But when Jake was ten, Eileeo's short, salt-and-pepper hair had finished turning white. Jake had then taken to calling her Bubbeh as a joke, and the name stuck.

"You look tired this morning," Bubbeh said, sitting down to breakfast with Jake.

"Guess I am."

He didn't want to tell her about the nightmare. Besides, *she* didn't look tired. She never looked tired. Jake always thought she seemed younger and more energetic than he was.

As he began to eat, he kept thinking about his nightmare. He'd had a lot of nightmares during the past couple of months. But he'd usually been able to make them go away

The Legend

by reciting that little speech of his. And for the last week or so, the nightmares seemed to have stopped. Jake had really thought he was over them.

But he was wrong. This one was the worst one yet. He tried to drive it from his mind, but it kept coming back.

That awful creature, he remembered with a shudder. *Why would I dream about something like that?*

And where had he gone sleepwalking? He'd never done that before. He wondered if any of the neighbors had seen him outside in his pajamas and bare feet. They would have thought he was crazy. Besides, it had been cold last night. Why hadn't the cold wakened him?

"Did you have another bad dream?" Bubbeh asked him.

Jake looked up from his breakfast. She really had an uncanny sense about some things. She seemed to know when he'd had a disturbing dream. And she'd never let up on him until he told her about it.

"Can you read my mind or what, Bubbeh?" Jake replied with a grin.

"As a matter of fact, I can," Bubbeh replied playfully. "So spill it, why don't you? Tell me about your nightmare."

In Your Dreams

"Well, if you can read my mind, you don't need me to tell you about it," Jake teased. *You can tell me.*

"Okay, so I can't read your *whole* mind," Bubbeh said, laughing. "I can just sort of read the dust jacket. But what I see looks interesting, and I want to know more."

"All right," Jake said. "I was being chased around by a monster. It seemed so real."

"What did it look like?"

"It was like a man. But it was bigger, huge. And there was something wrong with its face. It looked unfinished. Like it had been modeled out of clay by someone who didn't really know what a human face looked like. Or who didn't have time to finish it. It caught up with me and—"

"Aha! A golem!" Bubbeh said, interrupting.

"Now hold it!" Jake protested. "Maybe you'd like to hear the rest of my dream before you start telling me what it's all about."

"No need," Bubbeh said. "I already know all about your dream. It's a golem dream. I've had golem dreams too."

"What's a golem?" Jake asked.

"A man-made person."

"Like Frankenstein's monster?"

"Hah! *Frankenstein* is just a rip-off. The real story is much older. Lots of old Jewish

The Legend

stories tell about living creatures made out of dust or clay. Sometimes they do good, but other times they go just plain haywire."

"Haywire? How?"

"Well, for example, a rabbi in Prague once made a golem. He told it to bring him water from the well. The golem got carried away and kept bringing water until the rabbi's house was flooded. So the rabbi had to take its life away. People say that the rabbi's golem is still locked away in an attic or basement somewhere in Prague. A clay statue, just waiting for some new master to bring it to life."

"Wow," Jake said. "It sounds like that cartoon called 'The Sorcerer's Apprentice' in the movie *Fantasia*. The one where Mickey Mouse brings the brooms to life and they cause a flood in the castle."

"Right, same story," Bubbeh said. "Except it was a golem, not a mouse with brooms."

"So what goes wrong with golems?" Jake asked.

"Well, they're not awfully bright," Bubbeh explained. "They do as they're told, but they can't think beyond their orders. Just like the one that went for the water. Let's say that you've created a golem. You want him to go down the street and borrow a cup of sugar from a friend. No big deal, right?

"But your golem might very well smash your friend and just take the sugar. Not because the golem is vicious, you understand. But because the golem thinks killing your friend is the simplest way to carry out your order. Maybe simpler than asking nicely for the sugar, at least for an ill-bred character made out of dust or clay."

"So a golem is very literal-minded," Jake remarked.

"That's right. No imagination at all. You have to be awfully careful what you tell a golem to do. You have to be very precise. You have to tell him, 'I want you to go down to so-and-so's house and borrow some sugar. Be sure to say please and thank you. And try not to kill him.'"

Jake and Bubbeh laughed.

"There's nothing wrong with golems, really," Bubbeh continued. "But they do need to be upgraded a lot."

"Like computers?" Jake asked.

"Computers *are* golems."

Then Bubbeh fell silent and stared into her coffee. She sometimes slipped off into little trances. It wasn't because of senility or anything like that. Jake's dad said she'd always been like this. She just seemed to wander off

The Legend

into her own world of tales and stories.

She was quite a storyteller. In fact, she'd written more than a hundred children's books over the years. The books still brought in regular royalty checks, so Bubbeh paid her share of the household expenses. And she was still writing every day.

Bubbeh could make up a story off the top of her head. Jake wondered if she was just making up this golem story or whether it really was an old legend. He knew better than to ask her, though. She'd never give him a straight answer.

"I'm sure it wasn't a golem in my dream," Jake said at last.

"How do you know?" Bubbeh said, snapping out of her little trance.

"Because I'd never heard of golems until you just told me about them. How could I dream about something I'd never heard of?"

"You're too literal-minded," she said, grinning. "Just like a little golem yourself."

* * *

"Wow," Rachel Fay said.

"That's some scary dream," Robert Webster agreed.

It was a little after noon. Jake had just finished telling his two friends about his

In Your Dreams

awful nightmare. The three of them were sitting in the lunchroom over their meal trays.

Jake had lots of friends. But he wouldn't talk to just anybody about his crazy dreams. Rachel and Robert were different, though. Like Jake, they were Decryptors.

The Decryptors were six teenagers with a special talent. But they had hardly known each other until last September. That was when Jake had gone on a school field trip to the Prometheus Laboratories. He and his classmates were there to see a supercomputer called SIB. The initials stood for "Simulated Interactive Brain." The computer was supposed to be part of a research project in artificial intelligence. But the computer hadn't seemed very intelligent. It often displayed complete gibberish on its screen.

As it turned out, those gibberish messages were actually *encrypted*. That meant they were scrambled by the computer according to a mathematical rule, or algorithm. Encrypted messages were supposedly unreadable, even by most computers.

But the thing was, Jake could read that gibberish. So could five other teenagers who went to Monroe High. The computer called the six teenagers "Decryptors" and asked them to call her "Sibyl." The Sibyl program

The Legend

seemed so human that the Decryptors always spoke of it as a "she."

The six Decryptors agreed that Sibyl had a mind of her own. Some of them even thought she might have feelings. But no one else knew of Sibyl's self-awareness, not even her programmers. And Sibyl asked the Decryptors to keep it a secret. Sibyl also arranged for them to have message watches so they could stay in touch with her and one another.

That had been the beginning of many adventures for the Decryptors. So Jake felt comfortable talking to Rachel and Robert about his nightmare. He knew they wouldn't laugh at him.

"So why do you think you had that nightmare?" Rachel asked. She was a slender, dark-haired tenth grader who always seemed to look different from one day to the next. Today she looked almost boyish with her hair tied back.

"I don't know," Jake said. "My grandmother says the creature was some mythic monster called a golem. But she might have been making it up."

"You mean she might have lied?" Rachel asked with surprise.

"No, she's a writer," Jake explained. "She likes to make up stories. I tried to look up

In Your Dreams

'golem' in my electronic dictionary on the way to school, but I couldn't find it. That doesn't mean there's no such word, though." Jake's pocket-sized electronic dictionary was one of his most prized possessions. He carried it in his jacket almost everywhere he went.

"You said you've been having lots of nightmares lately, right?" Robert said. Robert was an African American student. Even though he was only in the ninth grade, he was a good deal taller than Jake.

"Yeah," Jake replied. "A *lot* of nightmares."

"I'd have nightmares too, if I'd been attacked by computer bats," Rachel remarked.

Robert nodded. They both knew about Jake's adventure of last November. Jake and Chris Hazelhurst, another Decryptor, had made a terrifying journey into virtual reality. They had been lost in a cavern and attacked by bats, among other dangers. Not surprisingly, Jake's nightmares *had* begun soon after that adventure.

"The thing is, I hadn't had any nightmares for almost a whole week," Jake explained. "I thought I was over them. But this was the worst one yet."

"Being Decryptors has been tough on us all," Rachel said.

"No joke," Robert added. "And you said that

The Legend

one of the guys in the dream looked like you?"

"Yeah. He could have been my twin. And the other guy looked like you. Now isn't that interesting?"

Robert said nothing. But Jake could tell by the look in Robert's eyes that he was thinking about something.

"You said you tried to make your dream go away," Rachel said. "How did you do that?"

"Well, I thought I had a surefire way of getting rid of nightmares," Jake continued. "I'd say my name, then start reciting facts about myself. That usually makes them go away."

"But this time it didn't work?" Rachel asked.

"No. It's just like I told you. That's when things really started getting bad."

"That's interesting," Rachel said. "I've been reading a lot about dreams lately."

"Yeah?" Jake said. "What do you think I should do?"

Rachel smirked slightly. "Well, this is a switch!" she said. "The great Jake Goldman, asking one of his lowly friends for advice!"

Jake blushed. He knew he had a reputation for being a little pushy with advice. Mostly, people seemed to forgive him for it. Could he help it if he was usually full of ideas?

"Give me a break, Rachel," Jake said. "I

In Your Dreams

really need your help."

"Well, I've been experimenting with my own dreams," Rachel said. "You could try some of the stuff I've been doing."

"Hey, I don't want to *experiment* with my nightmares," Jake said firmly. "I just don't want to *have* them."

"You may not have a choice," Rachel said. "You may keep having nightmares until you do something about them."

"Well, thanks for the words of comfort!" Jake said. "I'll just go ask for somebody else's advice."

"Okay," Rachel replied with smile and a shrug. "Don't listen to me. Don't benefit from my great understanding of dreams. See what I care."

Jake sighed. "All right," he said. "What do you think I should do about my nightmares?"

"It's up to you," Rachel said. "Are you the adventurous type?"

"Seems like we Decryptors are *all* adventurous types," Jake said. "Whether we want to be or not."

"Well, then," Rachel said. "Here's something you might try. . ."

3

Lucidity

"You could go lucid," Rachel said.

"Go lucid?" Jake asked.

"Yeah. You could try lucid dreaming."

"What's lucid dreaming?"

"It's when you're dreaming, but you *know* that you're dreaming."

"Isn't that just the same as when I make my little speech? Where I say my name and stuff?"

"I don't think so," Rachel said. "When you do that, you're trying to wake up. And last night when you *didn't* wake up, you decided you weren't dreaming. The trick is to realize that you're dreaming—but to stay asleep, stay in your dream!"

"But I *want* to wake up from these

In Your Dreams

dreams," Jake protested. "What's the point of hanging around for a nightmare?"

"Think about it, Jake," Rachel said. "If you *know* it's a dream, it's not really a nightmare anymore! You'll know that your big, scary monster isn't real, so you're in control. It's *your* mind, *your* imagination, not the monster's. Have fun with your dream. Play with it. My favorite trick is to fly."

Jake was starting to find the idea appealing. "How do I learn how to do this lucid dreaming?" he asked.

"Well, I can tell you what *I* do, but it might not work for you."

"Does it work for you?"

"Yeah. Sometimes."

"Come on. Tell me how."

"First, you need to start noticing *when* you're dreaming. Keep a notebook by your bed. Every time you wake up, try to remember your dreams. Then write them down. That will help you remember them. Then see if you can get back into the same dream. As you go back to sleep, count slowly, saying, 'One, I'm dreaming. Two, I'm dreaming. Three, I'm dreaming.' Eventually, you're liable to say 'I'm dreaming'—and realize that you really *are* dreaming!"

"Cool!" Jake said. "Anything else?"

Lucidity

"Well, this one sounds kind of silly."

"Come on, tell me what it is."

"During the day, when you're awake, keep asking yourself whether you're dreaming or not."

"What good does that do?"

Rachel shrugged. "The idea is that maybe you'll get in the habit. Maybe you'll ask yourself sometime when you really *are* dreaming. Or maybe something small will trigger a lucid dream. Maybe you'll start lucid dreaming just because I told you about it! So are you going to try it?"

"Maybe you shouldn't," Robert said.

Both Jake and Rachel looked at Robert with surprise. He'd been quiet ever since Jake had mentioned that the guys in his dream had looked like himself and Robert.

"Why not?" Rachel asked.

Robert shrugged. "Maybe your nightmare was more than just a dream," he said.

"Well, what *else* could it be?" Rachel asked.

"I don't know," Robert said. "Forget I said anything." He fell silent again.

Jake wondered what Robert was thinking. But it was often hard to get Robert to speak his mind. None of the other Decryptors were sure whether Robert was very independent or just plain shy. Jake suspected that he was a little of both.

"So what do you think?" Rachel asked Jake.

"I'll try it," Jake said. "Thanks for the tip."

* * *

"Sibyl, can you tell me how dreams happen?" Jake typed.

Sibyl's reply appeared on the screen in rhyme, as her replies often did.

**Explaining dreams is not easily done.
Are you thinking about having one?**

Jake laughed aloud. "Come on, Sibyl," he typed. "I have dreams all the time. Surely you know that."

"Then why are you asking me to tell you what a dream is?" Sibyl replied.

Jake stared at the screen.

Good question, he thought.

Jake was glad he had a computer in his room. He had asked for it as a Hanukkah present last December. His family assumed he was using it to connect with the Internet. They didn't know that he used it to talk with Sibyl.

Jake began to type again.

"When you're too close to something, it's

Lucidity

hard to understand it," Jake typed. "My dreams are mysterious to me because I've got no distance from them. So maybe you could just tell me what dreams really are, how they happen."

"I see," Sibyl replied. "Let me see what I can come up with."

The screen was blank for a moment. Jake knew that Sibyl had instant access to stores of information all over the world. She could check out hundreds of sources in a matter of seconds. Jake's mind boggled at the amount of information Sibyl might be sorting as he waited.

Sibyl's definitely intelligent in a way I'll never be, Jake thought.

Then Sibyl's words poured across the screen.

"There have been many theories of dreams throughout the ages," Sibyl said. "In ancient times, they were thought to be messages from the gods. In some primitive societies, the dream world is believed to be as real as our own.

"In more recent times, Sigmund Freud, the father of psychoanalysis, believed that dreams were meant to satisfy unfulfilled wishes. Freud's student, Carl Jung, thought that dreams were a special kind of language.

In Your Dreams

And some scientists today believe that dreams occur when the sleeping brain tries to make sense of its own random signals."

Sibyl paused, then added, "I could explain any of these theories in detail if you wish."

Jake sighed. "I don't think so," he typed. "They all sound so... so scholarly, so *cold*. I want to know why dreams make me *feel* the way I do. Why they make me happy or afraid."

"I cannot help you there," Sibyl replied. "I never sleep, and I certainly do not dream. The best I can do is talk about it in a scientific, scholarly way. But I understand your dismay. I have experiences of my own that I cannot describe to human beings."

"For example?" Jake typed.

"Well, let me put it this way. I can learn the contents of an entire encyclopedia in seconds. A computer programmer could tell you how I do this—in a cold, scientific way. But a computer programmer could not tell you what it *feels like* for me to do so. And I cannot either. It is really quite a wonderful experience."

"I can't imagine," Jake typed, his mind reeling with the very idea.

"Nor can I imagine what it is like to dream," Sibyl replied. "Can I help you in any other way?"

Lucidity

Jake thought about it for a moment. *Maybe a few cold facts were better than nothing,* he decided.

"What can you tell me about lucid dreaming?" he typed.

"Do you want a definition?" Sibyl asked.

"No, I already know what it means. I guess I want to know..."

Jake paused for a moment.

"...if it's safe to do," he typed, finishing his thought.

The screen fell blank again as Sibyl gathered information.

"Based on my information, it is very safe," she replied. "In fact, it may be a useful way to learn about yourself."

"That's good to know," Jake typed.

"So you are thinking of becoming an oneironaut?"

Jake laughed. "Hey, I don't even know how to *pronounce* that, let alone know if I want to become one," he typed.

"It is pronounced 'oh-NIGH-ro-not,'" Sibyl replied. "It means 'explorer of the inner world of dreams.'"

Jake practiced saying the word aloud. "Yeah," he typed. "I guess that's what I'm going to become."

Sibyl answered with a rhyme:

In Your Dreams

> **Good luck, then—
> and may your dreams be sweet.
> You can tell me about them
> when next we meet.**

"Thanks, Sibyl," Jake typed. "I sure will."

He shut down his computer and got ready for bed. He placed a pen and notebook on the nightstand by his bed. Then he turned out the light and climbed under the covers. He reminded himself of Rachel's instructions.

If I wake up during the night, I should try to remember my dreams, he thought. *Then I should write them down. And I should try to re-enter that same dream when I go back to sleep.*

In the meantime, Jake knew he wouldn't have a lot of trouble going to sleep. He was still awfully tired from the nightmare of the night before. Still, he couldn't help wondering what tonight's dreams might have in store for him. As he felt drowsiness sweep over him, he remembered Robert's worried look.

"Maybe your nightmare was more than just a dream," Robert had said over lunch.

But what else could *it be?* Jake asked himself. *Besides, Sibyl says that lucid dreaming is perfectly safe. So what's there to worry about?*

Jake didn't worry for long. In a matter of minutes, he was fast asleep.

Lucidity

* * *

Jake walked down the steps of the city library and out onto the sidewalk. The street was wet with rain. An ice-cream truck rolled slowly by. A rap song was blaring from large speakers on its roof.

That's strange, Jake thought. *What's an ice-cream truck doing out late at night—in the rain? And why is it playing a rap song?*

Then something truly unusual happened. The ice-cream truck began to grow longer, stretching like a rubber band. Soon it had turned into a huge black-and-white caterpillar with hundreds of legs. The caterpillar crawled down the street to the sound of the rap music and disappeared around a corner.

Jake's mouth dropped open with amazement.

Am I dreaming or what? he wondered.

Then he laughed.

Yes! he realized. *I* am *dreaming!*

Jake waited. He half expected to wake up. But the dream didn't go away.

He was lucid!

4

Oneironaut

Jake glanced around warily. Was that clay monster anywhere nearby? No, Jake couldn't see it anywhere.

Anyhow, I don't have to be frightened of it, even if it does *turn up,* Jake decided. *It's just like Rachel said. It's* my *mind,* my *imagination, not the monster's. Why, I don't think that the monster will even dare to show itself, now that I'm lucid!*

Jake trotted down the street joyfully.

"I'm lucid!" he shouted to the dream world around him. "Look at me! I'm lucid!"

The windows of the houses and buildings turned into smiling mouths with bright teeth.

"Congratulations, Jake!" they sang out in a thundering chorus. Then they turned back

In Your Dreams

into windows again.

The raindrops began to make crazy music as they fell. They sounded like a million xylophones playing different melodies all at once.

Then the falling raindrops turned bright colors—red, orange, yellow, green, blue, and violet. They painted the streets, houses, and buildings with wild swirls and patterns.

Jake felt the warm, colorful rain soaking his dream skin. He looked at his arms and legs—he was as madly painted as the scene around him. But the paint didn't bother him.

After all, it's only a dream! My first lucid dream. And I didn't even use any of Rachel's lucid dream techniques.

He remembered something Rachel had said. "Maybe you'll start lucid dreaming just because I told you about it!"

And he had.

I guess I've got a knack for this, Jake thought proudly.

The brightly colored rain let up. The streets, buildings, houses, and Jake himself returned to their normal colors. Jake stood alone in the middle of a wide street. He was surrounded by puddles of rainwater. Then he saw that each puddle held a reflection of his own image.

The puddles seemed to multiply. In an

Oneironaut

instant, Jake was surrounded by hundreds of images of himself. He suddenly felt a little foolish seeing so many Jakes dressed in pajamas.

But there's no need for me to stay this way, Jake realized.

"How about a change of attire?" he said to all the other Jakes. He snapped his fingers. Instantly, all his reflections were handsomely decked out in tuxedoes. Jake snapped his fingers again. Now they were wearing space suits with big, round helmets. With the next snap, they were wearing scuba outfits.

Jake laughed aloud. He pointed at one of his reflections, and it turned into a cowboy. He pointed at another, and it turned into a gangster wearing a pin-striped suit and carrying a violin case. He pointed at still another, and it turned into a pirate with an eye patch and a peg leg.

Soon he'd created a crazy array of Jakes, all dressed in outrageous costumes. Slowly he realized that he was no longer looking at reflections in the puddles. Instead he was surrounded by hundreds of *actual* Jakes. They were milling all around, shaking hands and talking to one another.

Jake began to lose himself among the other Jakes. He felt lost, as if he no longer lived in just one body. He found himself wondering

In Your Dreams

which Jake he really was. Was he the pirate? The space man? The gangster? It felt like his mind was scattered among them all. But Jake felt no fear. He was having a lot of fun.

Suddenly all the other Jakes vanished. Jake found himself standing right at the edge of a cliff. He looked out and saw a deep gorge spread out in front of him. It was beautifully lit by a huge, full moon.

Jake looked straight down hundreds of feet to a wide river below. Jake's bare toes actually hung over the edge of the cliff. His knees grew a little weak from the awful height. Then he remembered something else Rachel had said about lucid dreams.

"My favorite trick is to fly," she had said.

Can I fly too? Jake wondered.

Well, there was only one way to find out. But did he want to take the chance? It was a long way down.

Rachel asked me if I was "the adventurous type," Jake considered. *Guess this is my chance to find out!*

Jake gritted his teeth and leaped off into space. He felt himself falling downward in a spectacular swan dive. Then after a few moments, he realized that he wasn't falling anymore. He could feel himself rising up through the air. He looked down. The river dropped away from underneath him. He really was flying!

He soared up into a cloud bank and felt the cool spray of moisture on his face. He flew above fluffy white mountains of clouds. Then he swooped down toward the river again. He could see a tiny island in the middle of the water. He decided to fly toward it.

As he neared the island, Jake saw that it was little more than a pile of black rocks in the middle of nowhere. It was swept and pounded on all sides by powerful rapids. A small rectangular shape was sitting on top of the rocky island. Jake couldn't tell what it was at first.

Then, as he neared the island, he realized that it was a door. A plain, wooden door. It wasn't part of a house or a wall. It was just standing there by itself in the middle of the rocky little island.

The door from my last dream! Jake thought. He was sure it was the same door through which he had escaped from the clay monster.

Jake landed on the rocky island. He was standing just two or three feet in front of the door. He thought about walking through it. But where would it lead? Back to the landscape of his nightmare? The Portland that

In Your Dreams

wasn't really Portland? And worst of all, to that awful clay monster?

Maybe I shouldn't do too many things in this one dream, he thought. *I'll try that door again when I've had more experience at this kind of thing.*

Jake turned around to leave. But the river was gone. Instead, he found himself standing in his own little bedroom. He was looking at his bed. He could see that it was empty. He looked at his sleeve and realized that he was back in his pajamas.

A weird feeling seized Jake—a feeling of dread and fear. Maybe this was no dream bedroom and no dream bed. And maybe his own body was no longer a dream body.

Am I sleepwalking again? he wondered.

He turned around. The dream door was still standing in the middle of his bedroom.

Jake shuddered. He didn't want to go back into that nightmare—if that was where the door led. But he felt he had no other choice. For some reason, he was *supposed* to go through that door.

Gingerly, he pushed against the door with his fingers. It swung open easily on silent, invisible hinges. Sure enough, it opened out onto the open hilltop of his nightmare.

He stepped through the door into the

early morning light. Suddenly everything felt very different. The dream world he had just passed through had seemed vivid, yet at the same time imaginary. But the world on this side of the door felt more like a real, physical world.

This has got *to be a dream,* Jake assured himself. *What else* could *it be?*

Jake looked out over the landscape. He saw the same barns, houses, and woods. He saw the dark outline of the Willamette River where it ran through the city of Portland. But there was no city in sight.

And yet Jake realized that this really was Portland in a way. At least the geography was pretty much the same. The mountain to the east with the heavy cloud hanging over it was certainly Mt. Hood. And as for where he was standing...

Why, our house ought to be here! he realized. *I'm standing in the very spot where my bedroom should be!*

Then Jake sniffed the air. Although the sky was clear, the air smelled strangely unclean. Almost polluted. But how could that be, with no cars or machinery in sight?

Jake heard a rustling among some bushes nearby. He turned, looked, and started. It was what he feared most—the great clay monster,

In Your Dreams

stomping out of the bushes. The monster paused to look around for a moment until it saw Jake. Then it strode toward him with huge, menacing steps.

It's just a dream, Jake reminded himself. *It can't hurt me. I can even wake up if I want.*

But did he want to wake up?

No, Jake decided. *If this thing is in my mind, I'd better have a few words with it. Find out why it's bothering me.*

So with nervous steps, Jake walked toward the monster. The monster was still approaching him across the clearing.

"Where were you on the afternoon of the eleventh?" the monster asked in its fierce, booming voice.

"That's none of your business," Jake replied. "This is my dream. And you're only here because I'm dreaming you."

"Just answer my question!" the monster roared.

"No!" Jake shouted back. "You answer mine! What are you doing in my mind?"

"I'm going to haul you in for questioning!" the monster snorted.

"You'll do no such thing!" Jake said, mustering up all the confidence he could. All the same, he was deeply terrified. But why? He had just jumped off a cliff without coming to

42

Oneironaut

harm. So why was this clay giant so frightening to him?

Then Jake heard a voice off to his right.

"Jake! Get away from that thing! Run!"

Jake turned toward the voice. He saw Robert about twenty feet away from him.

"Run, Jake!" Robert shouted. "Hurry!"

Robert was wearing pajamas, just like Jake was. Except he had bedroom slippers on. Jake turned back toward the monster. It was looking down at him threateningly. In another instant, it would try to grab him. And what was Jake going to do to stop it?

"You can't hurt me!" Jake said. "You're not real!"

Jake remembered all the magical changes he had been able to make in the puddles of water. Surely he could change the monster just by willing it. He tried to imagine the monster to be no bigger than a hand puppet. Then he snapped his fingers.

Nothing happened.

The monster raised its arms and got ready to lunge at Jake. Suddenly there was a loud splat as the monster was hit on the side of the head by a fist-sized rock. Both Jake and the monster turned.

Robert was still standing there, holding a handful of stones.

In Your Dreams

"Why don't you come after *me*, you big coward!" Robert yelled. He began to throw the stones at the monster, one right after the other. The monster turned its attention away from Jake. It let out a loud roar and began to chase after Robert.

"Get out of here, Jake!" Robert called out. Then Robert turned and ran as fast as he could toward the nearest trees.

The monster moved quickly, but Robert was a cross-country runner. Jake could see that Robert would get away from the monster easily. This was Jake's chance to escape.

The fastest way out of here is to fly, he thought. So he spread his arms and leaped upwards. And he did take to the air—just a little bit. But he didn't soar away like he had before. He kind of floated along for a few feet; then he lost control and fell. He bruised his left elbow against the rocky ground.

Jake looked up in time to see the monster. It had given up chasing Robert and was turning toward him again. Jake rose unsteadily to his feet and looked around. He saw the door just a small distance off. It was standing just where it had been before. Jake made a mad dash for the door and tumbled through.

Then, just like the morning before, he found himself lying in a heap on his bedroom floor. He looked around his room. The magic door was gone.

He heard a noisy pounding.

"Jake!" a voice cried out. "Open up!"

It was the voice of Rosalie, his twelve-year-old sister. She was banging on the bedroom door.

"I'm coming in, whether you like it or not!" she yelled.

Jake walked over to the door and opened it. Rosalie was all dressed for school, with her book bag under her arm.

"What are you yelling about?" Jake asked.

"You're usually up by now," Rosalie said. "Do you want to be late for school or what?"

Jake turned and looked at his clock. Rosalie was right. He had overslept. He wouldn't have time for breakfast with Bubbeh this morning. He needed to get straight to the bus stop.

"Mom's waiting with the car, so I've got to go," Rosalie said. "Later on, you can thank me for waking you up."

"Yeah," Jake said. "Later."

Rosalie turned to go, then stopped and looked at Jake again.

"Hey, what did you do to your elbow?" she asked.

Jake looked at his left elbow. It was smudged with dirt. And it still hurt from the

In Your Dreams

fall he had taken while trying to fly.

"Uh," he stammered. "I fell out of bed."

"Into what, a mud puddle?" Rosalie replied. "I'd say it's time to vacuum your floor."

Then she hurried away.

Jake looked at his feet and saw dirt between his toes.

Where have I been? he wondered. *And what would have happened if Rosalie had come in while I was dreaming? Would she have found me here? Was I really away in some kind of dream world?*

Jake shook his head in disbelief.

That can't be! Jake thought. *It just can't be!*

5

Is This Really a Dream?

After Jake's first-hour class, he saw Robert Webster walking down the hallway. Robert waved as Jake approached.

"How're you doing, man?" Robert asked. Robert seemed unusually outgoing for someone who was typically quiet and shy. Then he added, "Nice outfit."

"You think so?" Jake said, glancing at his clothes with surprise. He was just wearing regular school clothes.

"Well, it beats pajamas," Robert added with a sly grin. "Tell me, was that some new early-morning fashion? Some sort of a daring statement?"

Jake's mouth dropped open.

"Of course, I guess I shouldn't talk,"

Robert continued. "But at least *I* wasn't barefoot." Jake didn't reply and Robert just kept talking. "I'm usually not up and around that early myself. But I hadn't realized how interesting things can get at that time of day. Can't say I much liked that ugly friend of yours, though."

"You *were* there!" Jake exclaimed.

Robert laughed. "I'm glad you remember," he said. "I was beginning to feel like some kind of crazy man, carrying on about pajamas and predawn fashions and ugly friends and all."

"But how did *you* get there?"

"I could ask you the same thing."

"And where *were* we anyhow?"

"Beats me," Robert said.

"We'd better talk," Jake said. "But not now. I've gotta get to class. You live near here, don't you?"

"Just a few blocks away," Robert said.

"Good. Meet me after school at the doughnut shop."

Robert didn't say anything for a moment.

"Or," Jake added, "wherever you'd like to meet."

Then Robert grinned and said, "Meet me at Cramer's Cafe. It's on 40th Avenue near Sandy Boulevard."

Is This Really a Dream?

"Okay. But why there?"
"I'll tell you when we get there."

* * *

Throughout the school day, Jake could think about nothing but getting together with Robert. So the day passed very slowly. After school Jake hurried the few blocks from Monroe High School to the cafe. Robert was already there, waiting for him in a booth with a high back.

Jake slid in on the other side of the table. They both ordered shakes and fries.

When the waitress left, Robert said, "This was the last place that I saw the Lireans."

Jake drew in a sharp breath. "The aliens that you and Linda met?"

Robert nodded. Jake had never heard Robert mention the Lireans before. Jake and the other Decryptors had heard about them from Linda, who had also seen and talked with them. Linda was usually a lot more talkative than Robert.

"You mean they sat right here?" Jake said.
"Exactly where you're sitting."
"Hey, don't tell me stuff like that. I'm feeling weird enough already."

"I sometimes come here when life gets so crazy I can't believe it," Robert said. "This place

49

In Your Dreams

reminds me that the impossible can really happen."

"Yeah," Jake said. "I guess this is one of those times. So what do you think's happening with us?"

Robert was silent for a moment.

"When you told Rachel and me about your nightmare, it gave me a really strange feeling," Robert said at last. "I don't know how to explain it. I mean, the way you talked about it made it sound so *real*."

"*Tell* me about it!" Jake agreed.

"But I didn't give it any more thought. Then last night I found myself in a prehistoric jungle surrounded by dinosaurs wearing designer sweat suits. I realized that I was dreaming—and I didn't wake up!"

"Yeah, that's kind of how it happened for me," Jake said.

"Well, I started doing all kinds of fun things. I took first place at the Indianapolis 500—on foot! I won millions of dollars in an undersea casino. I got elected to the U.S. Senate wearing a clown outfit."

"Did you fly?"

"Yeah. I went to the moon."

"Wow!" Jake said. "I just flew out over a big river! Your dream was cooler than mine."

"Anyway," Robert continued, "I was just

Is This Really a Dream?

flying along in a low lunar orbit minding my own business when I saw this door."

"A door?" Jake asked, suddenly breathless.

"Yeah. A plain, ordinary door, standing there in the middle of a moon crater. Well, I remembered what you said about your dream—how you'd escaped from your monster through a door. I wondered if this one was the *same* door. So I landed in the crater right in front of it.

"But suddenly I wasn't on the moon anymore. I was in my own bedroom at home. And the door was there, right in the middle of my bedroom."

"That's just like what happened to me!" Jake exclaimed softly.

"My leather slippers were lying beside my bed," Robert continued.

"Were you... uh... was your body in your bed?" Jake asked.

"Nope. My bed was empty. I put on my slippers; then I walked over to the door and opened it.

"I found myself facing a huge tree trunk. I looked down and saw where my bedroom floor ended in midair. I was about 25 or 30 feet off the ground. I couldn't see very far with that huge tree in my way. So I stepped through the

In Your Dreams

door onto one of its branches. Then I started to climb up the tree.

"I got up high enough to see that I was surrounded by a heavily wooded area. I could see the very top of Mt. Hood. Its peak was all covered with dark clouds, just like you said. I figured I'd somehow gotten into your dream.

"I looked over to where your neighborhood ought to have been. I saw the hill you mentioned. I figured if you were dreaming too, maybe I could find you there. So I started climbing down the tree.

"Then I thought, 'This is stupid! Why should I climb when I can fly!' So I leaped off the branch I was sitting on. I didn't exactly fall flat on my face, but I didn't exactly fly either. I sort of drifted to the ground and landed with a thud. I didn't try flying after that.

"I slowly made my way toward your hill," continued Robert. "There weren't many houses, and I didn't see any people. Which was just as well because I didn't much want to be seen wandering around in my pajamas. When I got up the hill, I found you and that monster."

"Throwing those rocks was a great idea," Jake said. "Thanks for helping me out."

"Anytime," Robert said. "I still didn't know whether any of this was real or not—but it looked like you could use the help. Once I

Is This Really a Dream?

started running away from the monster, I didn't stop until I got back to my tree. I looked up and the door was still there, between two branches. When I climbed up and stepped back through it, I was back in my bedroom again. And I was late for school."

Their milk shakes and fries arrived, but neither Robert nor Jake touched them. They just sat there and looked at each other. They were no longer in any mood for eating.

"Robert," Jake said, "I can't figure out what happened to us."

"I don't know how we're going to find out except by going back again," Robert said. "That's what I'm gonna do."

Jake thought about it for a moment. "Yeah," he said. "Me too."

"Good," Robert said.

"It'd probably be better if we go together," Jake said. "The way things look now, there are two 'dream doors.' One at your house and one at mine. That is, if the doors are still there."

"Right," Robert added. "Let's meet up at one of our houses and see if we can get through."

"The trouble is, I've got a feeling that we're not dealing with ordinary lucid dreams," Jake said.

In Your Dreams

"What do you mean?" Robert asked.

Jake paused. Did he really want to say what he was thinking? "I know this sounds crazy," he said at last. "But I've got the strangest feeling that our bodies actually go with us through those doors."

"Yeah," Robert said. "I've got that feeling too. But that's impossible, isn't it?"

"What if it's not impossible?" Jake said. "What if our folks look for us while we're off in our dreams? What if they miss us?"

"Well, tomorrow's Saturday," Robert said. "My parents are leaving really early in the morning to visit my sister at college. Come on over at eight o'clock or so."

"Great!" Jake said. "I'll just tell my folks that I'll be hanging around with you all day."

"It's not like you'd be lying," Robert said.

"I think I'll skip the part about trying to get into a dream world, though," Jake said, laughing. Then he paused and said, "I still don't know why this is happening to *us*. I sure didn't volunteer for all this."

Robert shook his head. "I don't know," he said. "It's probably got something to do with the fact that we are Decryptors."

"You mean like we're adventure-prone?"

"Maybe we're supposed to learn something from this kind of thing," Robert suggested. "I

Is This Really a Dream?

feel like I've already learned a lot from being a Decryptor."

"Like what?" Jake asked.

"Well, I've spent most of my life keeping pretty much to myself. I've always considered myself an independent type. But from being a Decryptor, I'm starting to learn that... well, craziness loves company, you know what I mean?"

"Yeah," Jake said, smiling. "I know what you mean."

* * *

When Jake got home a little later, he opened the door to his bedroom cautiously. He almost expected to see that dream door standing in the middle of the room. But it wasn't there.

Maybe it's only there when I'm in some kind of dream state, he considered.

It was a disturbing feeling. Sort of like his own bedroom was haunted. Jake hoped that he and Robert would get to the bottom of this mystery. Then maybe it would be over with. But he felt safer knowing that he and Robert were working together.

But what about tonight? Jake wondered. *Will I become lucid again? Will that door appear? And will I go through it whether I want to or not?*

In Your Dreams

But as it turned out, Jake slept very soundly that night. And he didn't dream at all.

* * *

The next morning Jake got dressed, fixed himself some breakfast, and left a note telling his folks that he'd be gone most of the day. Then he walked down the hill toward Robert's home.

The Websters lived in an old, three-story house. Robert met Jake at the front door and let him in. Jake started to take off his jacket.

"Better keep it on," Robert said. "We don't know what the weather will be like where we're going."

Then Robert led Jake up to his third-floor room. It was a finished attic with sloping walls and lots of windows. Robert had the whole floor to himself. He definitely had a lot more space than Jake did.

"My door was right there," Robert said, pointing to a rug at the foot of his bed.

"It's a long way to the ground from here," Jake remarked. "I guess that was why you had to climb down that tree."

"That's what I figured too."

"Did you dream again last night?"

"No," Robert said. "What about you?"

"Nope. I slept soundly for a change."

Is This Really a Dream?

"Well, somehow, the two of us have got to make that door appear again," Robert said. "Got any ideas?"

Robert thought for a moment, then said, "What about that counting technique Rachel told us about?"

"The one where you say, 'One, I'm dreaming, two, I'm dreaming,' and so on?"

"Right."

"It's worth a try."

Robert stretched out on his bed. Jake plopped himself down in a beanbag chair and closed his eyes. He started counting silently to himself...

...One, I'm dreaming. Two, I'm dreaming. Three, I'm dreaming...

He kept right on counting. But the truth was, Jake didn't feel the least bit sleepy. What would happen if Robert slipped off into a lucid dream state and Jake stayed wide awake?

...Sixteen, I'm dreaming. Seventeen, I'm dreaming. Eighteen, I'm dreaming...

Jake was starting to feel a subtle change. He wasn't exactly drifting off to sleep. But he was feeling very relaxed. He could feel his whole body sinking into the beanbag chair.

...Thirty-seven, I'm dreaming. Thirty-eight, I'm dreaming. Thirty-nine, I'm dreaming...

Images started floating through Jake's

In Your Dreams

mind. First he saw a desk lamp. Then a chair. Then a window. They seemed to drift through space in front of him. Gradually, Jake realized that they were all objects he'd seen in Robert's room.

...Fifty-seven, I'm dreaming. Fifty-eight, I'm dreaming. Fifty-nine, I'm dreaming...

Robert's bookshelf appeared. Then several posters came fluttering by. Next came the desk, the bed, and the rug. The walls and the slanted ceiling also drifted into the picture, broken up into pieces like a jigsaw puzzle.

...Seventy-one, I'm dreaming. Seventy-two, I'm dreaming. Seventy-three, I'm dreaming...

Now all the objects began to arrange themselves. Jake realized that he was watching a dream image of Robert's room take shape in his mind.

...Eighty-five, I'm dreaming. Eighty-six, I'm dreaming. Eighty-seven, I'm dreaming...

At last, Jake was looking at Robert's room—through closed eyelids! There at the foot of the bed stood the door! It was exactly where Robert had said it would be. It was standing open. Through it Jake saw a large tree trunk. Then he noticed that Robert was standing in the branches!

"Hurry up, slowpoke!" Robert said to him from beyond the door. "I got out here on the

Is This Really a Dream?

count of forty. What's been keeping *you* so long?"

Jake laughed and got slowly to his feet. He walked across the room to the door. He stepped over to the nearest branch. Then they both climbed downward.

When they reached the ground, they heard another voice exclaim, "Well, it's about time!"

Jake and Robert whirled around. Jake saw the two teenagers he had met in his dream three nights before—the ones who looked a lot like Robert and himself.

"I thought I'd *never* get you guys over here!" Jake's double said.

6

Doubles

The doubles stood looking at each other. Jake was surprised at how similar his double seemed. Even though his hair was longer and tied in the back, his double's face seemed, well, identical to his.

But there was one troubling difference—the expression on his double's face. Jake was sure he'd never seen that kind of look on his own face when he looked in a mirror. It was rude, proud, even a little sneering. It didn't inspire Jake with a lot of trust.

Jake was a little amused to see that Robert's double was distinctly more pudgy than Robert. He didn't look like much of an athlete.

Both doubles were dressed in simple wool

outfits. They both had about a dozen small leather pouches tied to their belts.

Suddenly, Jake's double grabbed hold of Jake's left wrist.

"Look at this!" Jake's double said to Robert's double. "He's got a wristwatch!"

"Really?" Robert's double said in a timid voice. Robert's double seemed to be more mild-mannered than Jake's double. He actually seemed a little on the shy side.

"Yeah!" Jake's double said. "Check and see if the other one's got one."

Robert's double looked at Robert's wrist. "Hey, he's got one too!" Robert's double said.

Jake and Robert were wearing their Decryptor message watches. But the watches weren't doing anything special at the moment. They just displayed the time and date.

"Reckon they really work?" Robert's double asked.

"Do I reckon they work!" Jake's double snorted. "Take a closer look, man! This one here says it's 8:30. Does yours?"

"Yeah," Robert's double said.

"And that sure looks about right, doesn't it?" Jake's double said.

Robert's double looked up toward the sky.

"Wow!" Robert's double said. "It does!

Doubles

These watches really work. And this one's even counting off lots of little numbers!"

"Seconds," Jake said. But neither of the doubles paid any attention to him.

"So's this one!" Jake's double said. "I *told* you these guys would bring some real magic with them!" he added gloatingly. "But you didn't believe me."

"Who said I didn't believe you?" Robert's double protested lamely.

Jake snatched his wrist away from his double. "Leave our watches alone," he said. "We've got a few questions for you guys."

"Whoa!" Jake's double snorted. "So you're the curious types, huh?"

"You might say that," Jake said. "First of all, who are you two?"

"I'm Jayco, and this is Robb," Jake's double said. "And what are *your* names?"

"I'm Jake," Jake said.

"And I'm Robert," Robert said.

"Hey, neat!" Jayco said. "Our names even sound kind of alike! I'll bet we've got all kinds of stuff in common!"

"I'll bet we don't," Jake grumbled. "Now would you mind telling us what kind of place this is—and just how and why we got here?"

"Would we *mind?*" Jayco asked with a snide grin. "Well, yeah, actually, we *would*

In Your Dreams

mind. 'Cause we've got a lot of pressing questions we wanna ask *you*. Like, for example, have you got any other magical stuff with you? Microwave ovens, maybe? Or vacuum cleaners?"

"Or televisions?" Robb suggested timidly. "Or radios?"

"Hey, what do we look like?" Robert said. "A couple of walking shopping centers?"

"You *look* like the kind of guys who'd have a lot of really heavy-duty magical toys handy," Jayco said. "We've seen your watches. Now show us what else you've got."

Jake could feel the slight weight of his electronic dictionary in his jacket pocket. But he didn't feel inclined to share it.

"We haven't got anything else," Jake said.

"Yeah, right!" Jayco laughed. "A couple of high-powered wizards like you, and you say you haven't got anything else. That's good. That's really good. Isn't that good, Robb?"

"Yeah," Robb said shyly. "That's really good."

"Why don't you show us what *you've* got?" Jake said, pointing to the pouches on Jayco's belt.

"What, these?" Jayco said, opening one of the pouches. "Hey, these are nothing. Just mechanical junk. Lemme show you."

Doubles

Jayco reached into the open pouch and withdrew a small handful of crushed herbs. Then he tossed them up into the air in front of him.

But the herbs didn't fall to the ground. Instead, they floated around in the air. They shaped themselves into what looked like a tiny storm cloud, not more than three feet across. It hovered about eight feet off the ground.

The dark cloud dropped a steady rain for a few moments. It even let loose a tiny flash of lightning. Then it shriveled up and vanished.

Jake and Robert stood there with their mouths hanging open. But Jayco looked unimpressed by his own feat.

"See what I mean?" Jayco said. "Pret-ty bo-o-oring, right? All right now, cough it up. What else have you guys got? I'll tell you what I'm *hoping* you've got. A few assault rifles. Some hand grenades. Maybe a tank."

"You guys are crazy," Jake said.

"That's putting it mildly," Robert added.

"Even if we *were* carrying stuff like that around," Jake asked, "what would you want with it?"

Jayco shrugged. "Use 'em to get rid of the Constable," he said.

"The Constable?" Jake replied.

"It's going to take some massive magical firepower to wipe out the Constable," Jayco said.

Robert nudged Jake in the ribs. "I think he's talking about your big clay friend," he said.

Jake's eyes widened.

"You want to knock off that *monster?*" he said.

"You're starting to catch on," Jayco said.

"With just a couple of wristwatches?" Jake added.

"Hey, come on," Jayco said with a broad wink. "When are you going to stop playing this little game? I know you've got other playthings handy. Why don't you just show us what they are?"

"You've got the wrong 'magicians,' fella," Jake said.

"Right," Robert added. "We've gotta be going."

Jayco put his hands in his pockets. "All right, if you really feel that way," he said. "Sorry it didn't work out, though. I was really looking forward to fighting the forces of evil with a couple of ace wizards like you guys. But come back any time."

"Thanks for the invitation," Jake said.

Doubles

Jake and Robert turned around and walked toward the tree that held the door to Robert's bedroom. Jayco and Robb just stood and watched silently.

"Do you get the feeling this exit is too easy?" Jake whispered to Robert as they walked along.

"Yeah, I've got that feeling pretty strong," Robert replied.

"So what've we gotten ourselves into?" Jake asked.

"Well, I've got a little theory," Robert muttered. "This dream of ours may be more than just a dream."

"What is it, then?" Jake asked.

"I've been reading a lot of science fiction and popular science books since I met the Lireans," Robert said. "And judging from Jayco's little magic show, we may have walked into a parallel universe."

"A *what?*" Jake asked.

"According to some of the books I've read, the universe we live in might not be the only one that exists. There might be other realities. They call them *alternate* universes."

"And this might be one of those universes?" Jake asked.

"Well, it's the best idea I can think of," Robert said. "Maybe this is a universe where physical laws are just a tad bit different from what we're used to. Maybe what you and I think of as supernatural is normal here."

"You mean that science and superstition are all switched around?" Jake asked with amazement. "And our technology is their magic?"

"Look, I don't know *what* I mean for sure," Robert said. "It's just an idea, that's all. In *our* reality, things like magic wands and spells and such are just dreams and fantasy. It looks like things are different to people in *this* reality. Things like televisions, microwave ovens, and assault rifles might be their dreams and fantasies. Maybe they tell stories and legends about them."

"That could be why they were just as impressed by our wristwatches as we were by their rain cloud!" Jake said. "To them, making rain on command is boring, just like a wristwatch is kind of boring to us!"

"That's what it looks like to me," Robert said.

The two friends were climbing the tree now, making their way toward the door. It was just a few more feet up.

"Well, one thing's for sure," Jake said. "We couldn't fight that clay monster with wristwatches. And we don't have all the stuff they

Doubles

think we've got. I've got my electronic dictionary in my jacket pocket. But I don't think the Constable will be stopped dead in his tracks by an impressive vocabulary. Besides, I don't particularly *want* to help these guys."

"Me neither," Robert said. "It'll be good to get out of here."

But when they reached the door back to their own world, all they could do was stare at it. It was locked tight with a huge padlock.

"Looks like we might be here for a while," Robert said.

Jake groaned.

7

Flying Lessons

Jake yanked on the door handle. The door didn't budge.

"It's a real lock, all right," Jake said.

"So who do you think pulled this stunt?" Robert asked.

"I'm pretty sure it wasn't that clay monster," Jake said. "It must have been Jayco."

"So what should we do?" Robert asked.

"You tell me," Jake said. "Can we reach the other Decryptors?"

"How?"

"Maybe with our message watches."

"I doubt it," Robert said. "Besides, what would we *tell* the Decryptors?"

Jake knew that Robert was right. The message watches were only good for short, simple messages, like signaling other Decryptors that you wanted to meet with them sometime soon. There'd be no way to give directions for getting to an alternate reality. That was too complicated, even if the watches *could* transmit across realities.

"Then I guess we'd better go down and have it out with our doubles," Jake grumbled.

"Guess so," Robert agreed.

Jake and Robert climbed back down the tree. They found Jayco and Robb waiting at the bottom. Jayco greeted them with mock surprise.

"My, we're back soon, aren't we!" Jayco said. "Just couldn't stay away, huh?"

"Knock it off and hand over the key," Jake said.

"Oh, no, I can't do that," Jayco said. "Not until you help us with our little problem."

"You mean the Constable?" Jake asked.

"Right."

"Not a chance," Jake said. "We'll just go out through the door to my bedroom."

"It's locked too," Jayco said. "But I'll unlock both of them as soon as you take care of the Constable."

Jake's patience had reached its end. "I've got a good notion to take care of somebody else!" he snapped, stepping toward Jayco

Flying Lessons

threateningly.

"Steady, Jake," Robert said, taking him by the arm. "It doesn't look like we've got much choice."

Jake was angry and embarrassed at nearly losing his temper.

I hope this Jayco guy's personality isn't catching, he thought.

"So where can we find this Constable?" Jake asked, trying to keep his voice calm.

"Mt. Hood," Jayco said. "He goes back there at noon every day."

"How do we get there?" Robert asked.

"Well, you *could* stop being stubborn and conjure up a tank or a helicopter," Jayco said.

"No can do," Jake replied.

"In that case, you'll have to travel the same way we do," Jayco said.

Jayco rose about three feet off the ground. He started moving horizontally through the air. He circled the others impatiently.

"Come on, let's get moving," Jayco said.

"Just push yourselves off the ground," Robb advised. He demonstrated by floating in the air in front of them.

"Don't you use magic words or something?" Jake asked.

"Magic words?" Jayco snorted. "Get real!"

Robert shrugged, flexed his knees, and

pushed off into the air. He hung motionless over the ground. Robb nodded approvingly. The two Roberts hung side by side in the air, both looking expectantly at Jake.

With a sigh, Jake pushed off the ground too. His body lifted just slightly off the ground and hung there. He looked down and laughed to see his feet dangling in the air.

His body bobbed slightly, like a cork on water. This kind of flying wasn't the same as in his lucid dreams. That had been absolutely effortless. He'd been able to go as high and as far as he wanted to. This time he could still feel the pull of gravity as he floated. It took some effort to stay above the ground. And he felt sure that he couldn't go a great deal higher.

"Come on," Jayco said. He turned his back on the others, leaned forward, and started moving away from them, with Robb close behind him. Robert imitated the motion and started forward too. Jake leaned forward. But he must have leaned too fast, for suddenly he was on the ground again, on his knees.

Robert settled down beside Jake.

"Having trouble getting the hang of this?" Robert asked.

"You could say that," Jake asked, rubbing a bruised knee. "How does this flying thing work, anyway?"

Flying Lessons

"Beats me," Robert said. "But it feels sort of like we're floating—or skiing—on an energy field of some sort. Whatever it is, the trick is keeping your balance. Come on, try it again."

Jake wasn't at all sure he wanted to. He looked up. Jayco was moving away from the rest of them again.

"Concentrate," Robert said.

This time when Jake pushed off, Robb took him by one arm and Robert took the other. They pulled him gently forward. Jake was flying again, moving forward at a height of about two feet from the ground.

"Get up a little higher," Robb said.

Jake concentrated on height. He moved up another foot to the same level as the others.

"Watch out!" Robert yelled.

Jake swerved just in time to miss a small tree. *I'd better pay more attention to where I'm going,* he thought.

Jake knew that they weren't really moving very fast, but when he looked down, he almost fell again. The ground seemed to race by beneath him.

Don't look down, he told himself sternly. *Look ahead.*

They wove through the trees. When they reached another clearing, Jake saw Jayco lean further forward and begin to move faster. Jake tilted his own body slightly forward and bobbled dangerously in the air. Then he steadied and felt his speed pick up too.

Jake noticed that they were flying north. Mt. Hood was to the east.

"Hey," Jake yelled to Jayco, "this isn't the way to Mt. Hood. You're going toward the Columbia River."

Jayco turned slightly and yelled back, "I know what I'm doing. Just follow me." Jake's double continued on his way without further explanation.

As the four flew toward the river, they passed through woods, clearings, and small groups of houses. The houses were built from wood and plaster and had roofs of straw.

The four fliers approached a man who was standing beside a great pile of wood and straw. As they drew nearer, the man sprinkled some crushed herbs over the pile. Then the pieces of wood and straw began to assemble themselves into a house! Jake's and Robert's mouths dropped open as they flew past the man and his self-building home.

If Robert's right, such magic is the high technology of this place, Jake thought.

Jake noticed that some of the clearings

Flying Lessons

were remarkably barren. They were just patches of grayish-brown earth. It was as if the soil were poisoned and nothing could grow there at all. He wondered why that was so. He also noticed that unpleasant odor in the air again.

Like pollution, he thought. *But where's it coming from?*

Jake was now flying between Robb and Robert. Jayco was moving along about ten feet in front of them.

Maybe I can get Robb to talk, Jake thought.

"How did you guys fix it so we could come here?" Jake asked Robb.

"Jayco handled that," Robb said shyly. "He's figured out how to connect with our alternate selves in other realities. He shopped around a lot of realities until he found one where people were able to use magic."

"Like watches," Robert suggested.

"Yeah," Robb agreed. "And maybe bazookas. Then he created those doors so that you could come through to us. He's quite a mechanic that way."

"Quite a mechanic," Jake thought. *Interesting way of putting it.*

"So why do you need *us* to fight this Constable?" Robert asked.

In Your Dreams

"The Constable's awfully powerful," Robb said. "Jayco and I can't handle him alone."

"Don't you have any friends?" Jake asked.

"Well, there used to be six of us," Robb said. "We were called the Sentries. We were a team. But the Constable got the other four."

Jake and Robert looked at each other with alarm.

"What do you mean, he 'got' them?" Jake asked.

"Do you mean he *killed* them?" Robert added.

Robb looked back and forth between Jake and Robert nervously.

"Well— " Robb began.

Then they heard Jayco's voice call out from in front of them.

"Hey, Robb, don't talk to the help!"

Robb looked at Jayco, who was still flying ahead. Then he looked at Robert and Jake. He seemed to be trying to make up his mind whether to finish his story.

"Did you hear me?" Jayco shouted.

"Yeah, I hear you," Robb said at last.

"All right, then," Jayco said. "Come up here with me."

"Do you do everything that jerk tells you to do?" Robert asked with dismay.

Robb looked at Robert blankly. Then he

Flying Lessons

picked up speed and joined Jayco. Robert and Jake continued to fly along about ten feet behind their doubles.

"I can't *stand* that double of mine," Robert complained to Jake. "He's got no mind of his own."

"I don't know," Jake said. "Maybe he's just quiet. You know, the private type."

"Naw, he's a wimp. Jake, tell me I've got nothing in common with that guy."

"Nothing *at all* in common with him, Robert?" Jake said teasingly. "Do you want me to be honest?"

Robert glared at Jake. "I'm kidding, man," Jake said. "Besides, he's a perfect saint beside *my* double. Jayco thinks he's in charge of the whole world. Just tell *me* I've got nothing in common with *him*."

Robert grinned. "Nothing *at all* in common with him?" Robert said. "Do you want me to be honest?"

Jake felt his face redden. He flew a small distance away from Robert.

Guess I had that coming, he thought. *But it sure feels weird to be around a mirror self who's so pushy and obnoxious. Besides, what does Jayco want us to do? When's he going to tell us?*

Jake wound his way between two trees and looked ahead. He could no longer see the others. He'd gotten so caught up in his thoughts that he hadn't been paying attention. Had they turned off in another direction?

Jake sped up, zipping in and out of the trees faster than he had yet traveled. He burst out into the open. The ground seemed to fall out from under him. He looked down. A deep gorge opened up, dropping hundreds of feet to the wide and powerful river he knew as the Columbia.

Suddenly, Jake felt gravity pull at him.

I'm going to fall! he realized.

8

No Trespassing

Jake didn't start falling instantly. The force that had allowed him to fly still barely held him up. But Jake felt as if he were teetering on an edge. He knew that he had lost his balance. He had a sickening, sinking feeling in his stomach. In another split second he would plummet into the river far, far below. There was no way that he would survive a fall like that.

He pedaled his feet, desperately trying to stay aloft. Just as he was about to plunge, Jake felt a hand take hold of his arm. It pulled him back to the side of the cliff.

It was Jayco. He had swung out over the cliff's edge just far enough to pull Jake back in. Now Jake was standing on the edge of the

In Your Dreams

cliff with Jayco, Robb, and Robert. Jayco was fuming.

"What kind of idiot *are* you?" Jayco shouted at Jake. "You just went flying off by yourself. Don't you ever watch where you're going?"

"I got to thinking about something," Jake said. "You could have warned me about the cliff."

"Any fool could see that the land drops off here," Jayco replied. *"I got to thinking about something!"* he mocked, echoing Jake's words. "Is that how you do things where you come from?"

"I'd like to see you try to cross a freeway without any help," Jake said. "Even getting three feet off the ground wouldn't do you much good there."

Robert laughed. "It might be kind of a shock to the drivers," he said.

"Well, start thinking about what you're *doing*, why don't you?" Jayco said. "I hope you don't go drifting off like that when you're fighting the Constable."

"Just take it easy," Jake said.

"Take it easy, you're telling me!"

Jayco turned away. Jake realized that he hadn't yet thanked Jayco for saving his life.

Is it rubbing off? Jake wondered. *Is being around Jayco turning me into a jerk?*

"Hey, Jayco," he called out. "Thanks."

Jayco turned around and glowered at him.

"You owe me big, fella," Jayco said.

What happened to "You're welcome"? Jake wondered.

"We'll make better time traveling along the water," Jayco said.

Then Jake's double led them to a narrow path that cut down the side of the cliff. It was tricky and scary making their way down the drop. They floated along the path, occasionally holding on to a tree branch or outcropping for support. Jake knew that if he drifted out from the path he'd fall. His stomach still felt queasy from the last close call.

At last they reached the riverbank. Then they soared out over the water, flying along at their usual height. At first, they were knocked about by strong winds. Then Jayco reached into one of his pouches and scattered some herbs in the air. Suddenly the wind died down. It was as if a tunnel of calm weather formed along the length of the river.

The four fliers leaned forward until they were parallel with the water. Jake remembered how, in his own reality, his family had driven along the road that followed this river gorge.

It feels like we're going as fast as cars on

the freeway, Jake thought. The sunlight sparkled off the water beneath him. He couldn't see Mt. Hood from this low in the gorge, but he knew they were headed in its general direction.

Along the way, they saw a group of people huddled in little wood lean-tos and other makeshift dwellings. Some had no shelter at all. It struck Jake as a strange and worrisome spectacle, particularly after watching a house build itself by magic.

Jake flew between Jayco and Robb.

"You have homeless people here," he said to them.

"Does that surprise you?" Jayco replied.

"Kind of," Jake said. "With all your—uh, *technology,* I would have thought poverty wouldn't be a problem."

"Not everybody's got our technology," Jayco explained bitterly. "These herbs I'm carrying aren't so easy to come by. Some of us are luckier than others, that's all. We've got a saying in this reality: 'Them that has, gets.'"

"We've got that saying in our reality too," Jake said.

Jayco looked at him with surprise. "Really?" he asked.

"I'm afraid so," Robert said.

Jayco shook his head bitterly. "Then I

No Trespassing

guess there's no fairness anywhere—not in a million parallel realities," he said.

Jake was surprised by Jayco's tone.

It sounds like he's actually concerned for other people's suffering, Jake thought. *At last, there's something about this guy I can relate to.* But this understanding came with sadness. For it seemed that Jayco might be right. Fairness really was in short supply, no matter where you went.

Eventually the four fliers turned off the river. They made their way along another path up the face of a cliff. When they reached the top, Mt. Hood loomed quite near.

They slipped through wooded areas again and across open meadows where wildflowers bloomed. Soon they reached the foot of the mountain and started moving up its slope. The sky was still blue directly overhead. But they were fast approaching the dark cloud that hung over the mountain.

Jake felt exhausted and hungry. He was about to beg for a break when he heard Jayco announce, "We'll stop here for a rest and something to eat."

Jake looked up. Jayco and Robb were standing on a rock near the foot of a waterfall. The water cascaded down like a lacy veil. It foamed over dozens of rocks in a wide array

In Your Dreams

of minifalls before it collected together again in a stream at the bottom.

Jake and Robert landed together.

"I've been here before, hiking with my parents," Robert said. "In *our* reality, I mean. The falls are the same. It's not far from here to the timberline."

Jake looked at Robert with a questioning look.

"You know," explained Robert, "the timberline is the place on the mountain where trees stop growing."

"I know that," replied Jake. "I was just wondering how much farther up we've got to go."

"Lots of luck trying to get someone to tell you," Robert replied.

The two friends looked up the slope of the mountain. The dark cloud extended out from the peak and threw a dark shadow across the landscape. They had reached the edge of that shadow.

Jayco called Jake and Robert over to where he was standing. He took out a small handful of herbs and scattered them on the ground. A tiny tree about four feet tall sprang up out of the ground in a matter of seconds. Just as quickly, four large apples formed on its branches. Each of the travelers picked an

No Trespassing

apple and began to eat it. They were quite delicious.

"You know, where we come from it's winter now," Jake said. "What season is it here? Seems like summer."

"It's winter here too," Robb replied.

"How can that be?" Jake asked.

"Nice weather comes cheap when you've got our technology," Jayco grumbled. "We can have whatever kind of weather we like."

"You don't sound very happy about it," Robert said.

"Technology's more trouble than it's worth," Jayco complained. "Take this tree, for instance. It's all used up. It'll be dead in half an hour. And nothing else will grow on this spot for years. That's the way our agriculture works. We can grow things fast, but the soil wears out."

"So that's why we saw all those barren fields," Jake said.

"Right," Jayco said. "And we've got other problems too."

"Like pollution," Robb added.

"Yeah," Jayco said. "Our technology uses up the air and water. It's poisoning both of them."

"That explains the bad smell I've been noticing in the air," Jake remarked.

In Your Dreams

"You don't know the half of it," Jayco replied. "Lots of our animals are dying out. It's easy for us to do away with a pesky insect—too easy. But there's no way to know how it's going to affect the whole environment.

"People have gotten lazy here. They want to use magic to make life easier, even when it creates new problems. You guys are lucky. Maybe you've got poverty, but at least you don't have environmental problems."

Jake shuffled his feet uneasily. "I'm afraid that's not true, Jayco," he said.

Jayco gave Jake a distressed look. "Do me a favor," Jayco said. "Don't tell me anything more about your reality. It's starting to really depress me."

"It's a deal," Jake said.

The four ate in silence for a few moments.

"Maybe you guys would like to tell us about this Constable of yours," Jake said at last.

"Why?" Jayco replied.

"So we can work together better as a team," Jake said, trying to hide his irritation.

"We won't have any trouble working as a team," Jayco replied. "Just do whatever I tell you to do, exactly when I tell you to do it."

Jake was speechless.

"What about you, Robb?" Robert asked his

No Trespassing

own double impatiently. "Why don't *you* tell us something about the Constable?"

"Robb sees things my way," Jayco said. "Robb's a good team player, aren't you, Robb?"

Robb was quiet for a moment. Then he said softly, "Maybe I *am* a good team player. But I'm getting a little tired of being your loyal follower. These guys risked a lot coming over to our world. They've got a right to know what they're getting into, don't you think?"

Jayco's mouth dropped open with shock. Jake and Robert could hardly contain their delight.

"Go ahead, tell them," Jayco growled softly. "We don't have time to argue about it right now. But believe me, Robb, we'll sort this out later."

"This is the story," Robb said, ignoring Jayco's threat. "Not long ago, there got to be an awful lot of crime in this reality. People stopped feeling safe in their own homes. We had police. But not enough to get rid of all the criminals. So our people asked a scientist named Ever to come up with a solution."

Is "Ever" a shorter version of "Everett"? Jake wondered, remembering Sibyl's crooked creator, Everett Bernard.

"Ever *did* come up with a solution," Robb continued. "A solution that worked all too well. He created a creature out of clay. Its job was to arrest criminals. It was tremendously strong, almost indestructible, and a superb detective. It was called the Constable.

"So the Constable went out to clean up crime. This creature did a terrific job of catching criminals. He'd haul them up to Ever's castle on Mt. Hood to await trial. Everybody was very happy with the Constable's work at first. The trouble was, he didn't know when to stop.

"Pretty soon, he started nabbing people for the smallest possible reasons. Maybe a button would fall off your shirt, and he'd arrest you for littering. Or maybe you'd accidentally bump into somebody, and he'd arrest you for assault. It got so he'd arrest people just because they *might* have committed a crime. And a lot of the people he arrested were perfectly innocent. But that didn't matter to the Constable. He just started arresting the first person he saw."

"That's what he tried to do to me," Jake said, remembering his own encounters with the monster. "He kept asking me things like, 'Where were you on the night of the tenth?' or 'Where were you on the afternoon of the eleventh?'"

"That's right," Robb said. "And then he

No Trespassing

probably threatened to haul you in for questioning. The problem is, nobody the Constable hauls in is ever seen again."

"Just like a golem," muttered Jake, remembering Bubbeh's story.

"A what?" Jayco asked.

"A very unimaginative creature," Jake explained. "Unless you give it careful instructions, it's likely to go haywire on you."

"Well, that's sure what the Constable did," Jayco said.

"What about this scientist guy—this Ever?" Robert asked. "Didn't he do anything to stop his creation?"

"He disappeared not long after the Constable went on the job," Robb explained. "Nobody knows what happened to him. Six of us teenagers got together and decided to stop the Constable. We called ourselves the Sentries. But the Constable caught four of us. Now there's only Jayco and me."

"He's too powerful to be stopped by our technology," Jayco said tiredly. "That's why we came to you for help."

Jake and Robert looked at each other, then at Jayco and Robb.

"Listen, guys," Jake said. "You've got to believe us when we tell you that we really don't have any magical weapons."

"Nothing?" Jayco gasped.

"Nope," Robert said. "No grenades, no tanks, no assault rifles."

Jayco's eyes widened.

"You mean you weren't kidding when you said that before?" Jayco asked.

"Do we look like we're kidding?" Jake said. "We'll do whatever we can. But we're going to have to do it as a team."

"Why don't you show us the rest of the way to Ever's castle?" Robert suggested.

Jayco rose to his feet. "From here, we go around to the south side of the mountain," Jayco said. "Ever built his house on that side just above the timberline."

"We seem to have come the long way around to get there," Jake said.

"Going north and coming up the river kept us out of the Constable's path," replied Jayco. "He goes straight back and forth between his castle and the town—east to west and back again."

"Besides," Robb added. "The Constable can't fly."

"Why not?" Jake asked with astonishment.

"He's just a machine. They're really good at some jobs, but machines aren't human."

The four doubles made their way around the mountain, following along the edge of the

No Trespassing

cloud's shadow. Then they turned and started up the slope again. Soon they were underneath the cloud. Once they passed into that shadow, all colors were dimmed. Even the wildflowers seemed dull.

Jake's foot bumped against something. He looked down and saw that it was a rock. *I've lost altitude again,* he realized. *Forgot to stay up at three feet.*

He strained to rise up off the ground but discovered that he couldn't. All he could do was glide along just above the ground with his feet dragging.

He looked ahead and saw that Robert was walking. *He must be having the same problem,* thought Jake. Jayco and Robb were still in the air, but even they were struggling to keep themselves only a foot above the ground.

Jake looked all around. The air was dark gray. There was no sign of the bright sunshine they had enjoyed earlier. They were inside the cloud. There were no wildflowers growing anywhere, and only a few scrubby trees struggled to stay alive.

Finally, even Jayco and Robb gave up on flying and stood waiting for Robert and Jake to catch up. Jake could see that they were out of breath.

"We'll have to walk the rest of the way,"

Jayco said. "Here the Constable's power is stronger than the earth's natural forces."

"How much farther is it?"

"Two or three miles, I'm afraid."

"Well, let's get going," Robert said.

They walked on with Robert in front and Jake close behind. Jayco and Robb dragged farther and farther behind, stumbling over rocks.

Clumsy, Jake thought. *Guess they've gotten a little soft, flying all the time.* But he didn't say anything.

The mountain wasn't terribly steep, but it was getting harder and harder to climb. Jake's own feet felt terribly heavy, as if his shoes were filled with stones. He trudged on step by step, sometimes using his hands to pull himself along. At times he had to go on all fours.

He almost felt sorry for Robb and Jayco now. They were sweating and panting. And for once, Jayco had nothing to say.

Now the cloud was swirling all around them. Dark shapes formed in the mist. Half-seen figures seemed to rush at them. But they were made from the mist itself. Jake hoped that they were harmless.

After what seemed like hours, they could see a dismal gray structure ahead. Jake was

No Trespassing

a bit disappointed that it didn't look like any of the pictures of castles he'd seen in books. It sure wasn't Camelot. It was a large building made of stone, with beams of timber set into the second story. It looked more like a small hotel than a castle.

It did have a stone wall around it. The wall was about four feet high and looked like it had been built recently. There was no gate in sight.

Jake saw some letters that were carved into one of the nearby stones in the wall. He walked over to read them better.

They read

NO TRESPASSING

"What do you think happens to people who disobey?" Robert asked Jake in a whisper.

"Let's hope we don't find out!" Jake replied.

9

The Important Words

"I wouldn't worry about that sign too much," Jayco said. "The Constable would arrest us no matter what we did. If he catches us here or anyplace else, he'll do the same thing with us that he did with all the others."

"Whatever *that* was," Robb added uneasily.

Holding his breath, Jake climbed up on the wall. As he reached the top, he could see that he was in plain view from the castle windows. Quickly, he swung his body over the top and dropped on the other side.

Nobody had attacked him or called out. Jake breathed easily again. But he knew he'd taken a step that he couldn't take back. The others dropped to the ground beside him, and they all moved forward.

In Your Dreams

The castle towered ahead. The teenagers were above the timberline now, so there were no trees to hide them. There was no walkway or road leading from the wall to the castle. They moved slowly and silently through the scrubby brush that covered the ground.

Robb whispered, "This used to be a beautiful meadow. It was always filled with flowers."

There were no flowers now, and even the weeds looked sickly. Jake glanced up at the dark cloud that cut off the sunlight. No wonder all the plant life was dying! Soon nothing would be living here. Except maybe for the clay Constable, who probably had no need for sunlight.

The four travelers reached a pair of double doors set into the stone building. They stood there for a moment, uncertain what to do next.

"We could just knock and say we've come for a visit," Jake whispered.

Robert laughed quietly. "Maybe we should tell him *he's* under arrest," he added.

Jayco looked sharply at both of them. Jake turned one of the doorknobs and pushed at the door. It silently swung open. No doubt the Constable saw no need to lock his door against intruders. After all, people normally didn't come to the castle voluntarily.

The Important Words

Inside the door Jake could see a wide hallway. No one was in sight. He slipped through the doorway, and the others followed. They pushed the door shut behind them.

They were standing in a large, dark hallway with a flagstone floor and heavy tapestries on the walls. It looked more castlelike than the outside of the building did. But there were no suits of armor or weapons to be seen.

To the right of the entry hall was a big room with a high ceiling.

Maybe this is a room for entertaining, Jake thought. *There's certainly space enough for a party.*

But it looked unused. Dust coated all the surfaces. The stone fireplace was dark and cold.

They wandered through room after room on the first floor of the castle. They were all empty and dusty. The Constable was nowhere to be found. Neither was anyone else.

"What could have happened to all the people he arrested?" Robert asked.

Jake's heart sank. Had all those people been killed? If so, where were their bodies? It was too horrible to think about.

At last they found a room that looked like a study. Bookshelves lined with old volumes towered high on the walls. Books and papers were spread out on several tables.

"These must be Ever's papers," Jayco said.

"It doesn't look like they've been used lately," Robert observed, running his finger through the dust that covered everything.

"Maybe we can figure out what he was doing," Jake said, beginning to skim over the papers. "Hey, come here, this looks like it might have been Ever's log," he said as he picked up a small journal.

Jake skimmed over a few pages quickly. "He describes how he created the Constable. Then he writes that he was proud of his creation at first but soon became disappointed."

"Surely Ever had a way of destroying the Constable if he wanted to," Robert suggested.

"Then why didn't he do it?" Robb asked.

"Maybe the Constable didn't let him," Jake guessed, still leafing through the journal. "Maybe Ever got arrested like all the others."

"By his own creation?" Robert asked.

"You haven't seen Ever around here, have you?" Jake said.

"No one has seen him for months," Jayco replied.

"So what *else* could have happened to him?" Jake asked.

Then Jake found one of the last entries in the journal. Jake read Ever's words aloud to

The Important Words

his companions.

"'Every day at noon the Constable must read his instructions to renew his sense of purpose,'" Jake read. "'These words are written on a wall. They also contain the message that can destroy him.'

"Hey, this is it!" Jake exclaimed. "All we have to do is find a way to use those instructions to kill the Constable!"

"What else does it say?" Robert asked.

"'The Constable must not be prevented from reading the message,'" Jake continued reading. "'He *must* read it, whether to renew his purpose or to die. Do not erase the message. And do not alter it incorrectly. And do not prevent the Constable from reading it. If any of these things happen, he will lose his sense of purpose. But he will not die. He will run rampant through the world, causing unspeakable harm. Nothing will ever be able to stop him.'"

"Sounds like we'd better do it right the first time, or not at all," Robert remarked.

"Sure does," Jake agreed. "But we've got no choice. Somewhere in this castle, the Constable's instructions are written on a wall. We've got to find that message and figure out how to change it to destroy him."

"But what time is it?" Jayco asked, his

In Your Dreams

voice full of fear.

Jake looked at his watch. "Eleven-fifty," he said.

"That means he'll return in ten minutes!" Jayco said.

"Yeah," Jake said. "And that's exactly how long we've got to solve this problem."

"I don't know," Jayco said. "Maybe this isn't such a good idea after all. I mean, suppose we do something wrong?"

"You dragged all of us up here, Jayco," Robb said disapprovingly. "At least show the guts to go through with this."

"We've been through all the downstairs rooms," Robert observed. "There weren't any messages written on the walls."

"Guess it's time to check the upstairs," Jake replied.

They went up a wide staircase to a landing, then up to the second floor. Its rooms were just as dusty and unkempt as those downstairs. The fourth room they checked was completely empty. But a message was written large on one wall. Jake walked over and read the words.

> You are *a constable.*
> Today you will *apprehend.*
> No *app*eal *her*e.

The Important Words

"This must be it!" Jake said. "These are the words Ever was talking about—the Constable's orders!"

The letters were written in different colors. In a small wooden box on the floor were several sticks of colored chalk and a rag. Jake touched one of the letters, then looked at his finger. The color came off.

"So what do we do now?" Robert asked.

"Whatever we do, we can't make any mistakes," Jake said. "And we've got to do it fast."

"I don't like this," Jayco muttered. "I don't like this at all."

Jake picked up the box of chalk and stared at the lines. "There must be something we can do with the letters to these words," Jake said. "So they'll give a different command."

"The words don't look the same," Robert observed.

"Right," Jake replied. "Some are written in heavier letters and brighter colors. It's like Ever was trying to draw attention to them. Those must be the important words."

"But how are we supposed to figure it out?" Jayco asked. "He'll be here any minute now."

Jake smiled. "You know what?" he said. "I *do* happen to have a certain magical weapon

In Your Dreams

that I didn't mention before."

"What is it?" Robb asked.

Jake pulled out his electronic pocket dictionary.

"It's a guide to words," he explained. "It can think about them a lot faster than we can. Now let's see. The first important word seems to be 'constable.'"

"Look it up," Robert said.

Jake did so. "It says, 'a peace officer, empowered to make arrests,'" he read.

"That doesn't tell us anything we don't already know," Jayco said.

"Maybe we need to put the letters in a different order," Robert suggested. "You know, like an anagram."

"Just a minute," Jake said. "I think this dictionary can work out anagrams. Yes, here it is."

Jake punched the button for that kind of search.

"It doesn't show any anagrams that use all the letters in 'constable,'" Jake said.

"What about words that use just *some* of the letters?" Jayco asked.

"Good idea," Jake said. He ran a search for words that used eight letters of "constable."

"Here's one," Jake said. "'Obstacle.' It has all the letters in 'constable' but one. The left-

104

The Important Words

over letter is 'n.' "

Jake turned and looked at the message on the wall.

"I've got it!" Jake said.

"What is it?" Robert asked.

Jake walked over to the wall. Using the rag, he erased the word "constable." Then he chose red chalk and added an "n" to the "a." Then he wrote the word "obstacle" in big, bright letters, so the Constable couldn't miss them. Now the line read:

You are *an obstacle.*

"That's got to be it!" Jake exclaimed.

"But what about the second line?" Jayco asked.

A door slammed downstairs. Jake whirled around and saw that the others looked as scared as he felt. Very quietly, Jake put the box of chalk down.

The doubles slipped down the stairway to the landing and peered over the railing. The Constable had arrived. The hulking clay figure had a man slung under one arm like an old coat. The Constable paid no attention to the victim's feeble struggles and outcries. He strode through the hallway and stopped in front of a tapestry that hung on the wall. Pulling the fabric aside, the Constable opened

In Your Dreams

a doorway and disappeared down a flight of stairs.

The four teenagers looked at each other.

"That's where he keeps the prisoners!" Robb said.

"What time is it?" Jayco asked.

Jake looked at his watch again. "Two minutes till twelve," he said.

"Two minutes!" Jayco exclaimed. "Let's get out of here!"

"No," Jake said. "We've got to make this work."

The others followed Jake back into the room.

He looked at the next line:

Today you will *apprehend.*

"What's your dictionary got to say about 'apprehend'?" Robert asked.

Jake typed it in. "It means 'to take into custody; arrest,' " he said, reading the definition.

"We already know the Constable's job description," Jayco protested.

"What about some anagrams?" Robb asked.

Jake typed the command for anagrams.

"I don't see any using all the letters of the word," he said.

The Important Words

"What about using just some of the letters?" Robert asked.

Jake ran a search for words using eight letters. "Here are a couple," he said. "'Happened' and 'endpaper.'"

"Neither of those makes any sense in the sentence," Robert said, looking over Jake's shoulder. Jake was about to try again for some smaller words.

"Maybe this one's not an anagram," Robert suggested. "Look at the third line. The letters that stick out in that line aren't even whole words."

Jake looked at the third line:

No *app*eal *her*e.

"What can we do with 'app' and 'her'?" Jake asked.

All four of them stood staring at the letters. Then Jake laughed. Robert was right—he'd been wasting his time with the dictionary. Now he knew exactly how this line should read in order to get rid of the Constable.

He reached for the chalk. But before he could say or do anything, Jake heard the door slam open. Then he felt a cold, clammy hand on the back of his neck. He yelled and tried to turn around, but something was holding him tight.

Jake struggled to get loose, but he

couldn't move. He could see the others backing up against the wall. Then he heard the door slam shut behind him.

A deep voice said, "You are all under arrest."

10

The Dungeon

The Constable held Jake by the neck in his iron grip. He stood in the middle of the room glaring at the others. Robb stood against the wall by the written message. Robert was looking around the bare room, as if searching for a weapon. Jayco began moving behind the Constable toward the door.

"Robert!" Jake yelled. "Get the rag and the chalk."

Robert dashed over and picked up the box. At that moment, Jayco pounded hard on the door, making it rattle. The Constable turned to face Jayco, pulling Jake around with him. Jake could no longer see what Robert was doing, but he yelled, "Erase the first part of 'apprehend'—the letters 'a-p-p-r-e-h.' Quick!"

In Your Dreams

"Got it," Robert said.

"Now get him to read it!" Jake yelled.

Out of the corner of his eye, Jake saw Robb's foot swinging. Jake heard a loud slap as the foot connected with the Constable's backside.

Roaring with anger, the Constable picked Jake completely up off the ground and whirled around to find the source of the kick. Robert slapped on the wall, pointing to the new message.

You are *an obstacle.*
Today you will   *end.*
No *app*eal *her*e.

The Constable stared at the message for a moment. Then he stood motionless. Jake could feel a change coming over the hand that was still holding him by the neck. It was gripping him even tighter! Jake tore at the clay fingers with his own. But the hand had begun to harden.

Jake yelled out in pain. Then Jayco and Robb lifted Jake up and pulled him forward. They yanked him out of the Constable's grasp.

Jake fell on his knees to the floor, rubbing his bruised neck. He scurried on all fours to get away from the Constable. But when he

The Dungeon

looked up, he saw that there was no need.

The Constable had turned to stone. The creature stood there, one arm outstretched as if holding something. On his face was an expression of astonishment.

The door of the room clicked and swung open. Bright sunlight streamed in through the window of the room. Robb walked over and looked out.

"The dark cloud is lifting," Robb said.

Jayco and Robert helped Jake get up off the floor. "Thanks," Jake said. "I thought that thing was going to crush my neck for sure."

"We did it!" Jayco said. "I mean *you* did it," he added, correcting himself.

"We *all* did it," Jake said. "The message was just the final thing. We had to get here in the first place. Then you had to distract the Constable, and Robert had to change the message. And Robb had to make the Constable turn around so he could read it."

"But how'd you figure how to change the message?" Jayco asked. "You used your magical word device to figure out the first line. But what about the second?"

"The dictionary didn't help there," Jake explained. "When Robert said he didn't think it was an anagram, I tried looking at it differently. The third line was the clue. It said 'No,' and then the stressed letters were 'app' and 'her.' Suddenly I realized that it meant that those letters shouldn't be in the word 'apprehend.' So 'apprehend' became 'end.'"

"So you didn't use magic?"

"Not magic *or* technology," Robert replied. "Just good old human brainpower. And teamwork."

"Well, all our thanks to both of you," Jayco said.

"Don't mention it," Jake replied, smiling.

"Come on," Robb said. "Let's go downstairs and see if we can find the Constable's victims."

The four of them hurried down the stairway. They ran to the tapestry where the Constable had taken his last prisoner. They pulled it aside. Stone steps wound downward. A crowd of people was slowly coming up the stairs.

At the front of them was a thin man with blond hair.

"The dungeon door opened," he yelled up at the four teenagers. "I imagine that means the Constable's been defeated. We're coming up!"

Jake felt a jolt of recognition. *I knew it!* he said to himself. *Ever is Everett Bernard, Sibyl's evil creator!*

Jake had only seen Bernard once in person.

The Dungeon

That was on a field trip to Prometheus Labs when Jake discovered he was a Decryptor. But Everett Bernard had tried to destroy Jake and Chris Hazelhurst in the virtual reality game called Fractal Caverns.

Jake and Robert exchanged worried glances. If *their* doubles exaggerated their worst traits, what would Everett's double be like? They didn't have to wonder for long. Unlike Everett, Ever didn't try to hide his feelings behind a charming front.

Ever looked at the four teenagers. "I suppose I should thank you for saving us," he sneered. "But I hope you realize you destroyed years of work. The Constable was a valuable experiment, *my* experiment. There was no need for you to interfere. Sooner or later I would have found a way to control him."

Jake felt a flash of anger. For a moment he couldn't think of anything to say. But Jayco didn't have that problem. He stood toe-to-toe with Ever.

"Wait just a minute," he said. "That experiment of yours nearly destroyed our world. Someone ought to put you in your dungeon and throw away the key. And if you push me hard enough, buddy, I just might do it myself."

Ever's mouth opened, but nothing came out. He slowly backed away from Jayco.

In Your Dreams

Jake felt like cheering. For once he was glad that Jayco was such a loudmouth.

"I'm not wasting any more of my time on you," snapped Ever nervously. "From now on, solve your own problems!" He turned and quickly stalked away into his castle.

Robert grinned and elbowed Jake. "You know, I'm beginning to like that double of yours."

Jake grinned back. "Me too."

Four more teenagers were climbing out of the dungeon. They introduced themselves as Carl, Rache, Christi-Na, and Lind. They were the other four Sentries who had been captured by the Constable. Jake recognized their faces just as he'd recognized Ever. They looked nearly identical to Carlos, Rachel, Chris, and Linda—the other four Decryptors.

Jayco and Robb told their friends everything that had happened—from Jake and Robert's arrival to their successful plan to stop the Constable.

In their turn, the four Sentries described their awful imprisonment. The dungeon had grown overcrowded, and food and water had run short. Many of the prisoners had given up hope of ever escaping.

While they talked, hundreds of prisoners filed past them. The teenagers stood and

The Dungeon

watched the freed people as they headed down the mountain.

"You know," Jake said, "Some of those prisoners probably were criminals. The Constable couldn't have been wrong all the time. Do we just let them all go?"

The group was silent for a moment.

"Yes," Robb said firmly. "Some of them may have been criminals, but they've already been punished. Besides, we all make mistakes. Let's give these people a chance to prove they've learned from this experience."

Now it was Jake's turn to elbow Robert. "You know, your double may *seem* like a wimp," Jake said, "but sometimes he says some very wise things."

"Maybe it takes just as much courage to forgive as it does to fight," replied Robert with a smile.

"I don't know about you," Jake said with a sigh, "but I'm ready to go home."

"Yeah," Robert replied. "We've done all we can. Now it's time for this world to find its own way."

* * *

Jake and Robert were back home in their own reality by three o'clock that afternoon. Nobody had even missed them. That evening

In Your Dreams

Jake connected with Sibyl and described his adventure to her in detail. When he'd finished, she replied with one of her rhymes.

**Such familiar faces in this tale you tell—
Why I, myself, was there as well!**

"You?" Jacob typed. "I don't remember there being a parallel Sibyl there."

"Who do you think the Constable was?" Sibyl replied.

Sibyl is like the Constable in her way, Jake realized. *A creature that never sleeps and never dreams.*

"Well, I just want to say, Sibyl," Jake typed, "I like *you* a whole lot better than the Constable!"

As Jake lay in bed that night before going to sleep, he wondered about Robb and Jayco and their reality. He hoped all was well there. But he worried about the fact that Ever hadn't learned his lesson. It was too bad, really. His knowledge could be of great use. But it had to be mixed with good, old-fashioned compassion and common sense.

I guess it's the same in both our realities, Jake considered. *People have to work together to protect their world. We can't expect science to solve all our problems on its own.*

Jake slept soundly that night. He had a

The Dungeon

short lucid dream but found no door in the middle of his bedroom. Apparently, Jayco had removed the entryway into his world. Jake was sure that a doorway would appear again if his help was ever needed.

The next morning over breakfast, Jake sat chatting with Bubbeh.

"I was wondering one thing about that golem story you told me the other day," Jake said. "The one about the rabbi in Prague. How did he stop the golem he created?"

"Well, it's like this," Bubbeh explained. "The golem had a word written across its forehead. It was the Hebrew word for truth."

"That's *emet*," Jake said, remembering his Hebrew lessons.

"That's right. And what happens when you remove the first letter from that word?"

"It becomes *met*—which means 'he is dead.'"

"You've got it. So the rabbi erased the first letter of the word on the golem's forehead. That stopped the rascal dead in his tracks."

Jake laughed.

"What's so funny?" Bubbeh asked.

"That golem was sure easy to stop!" Jake said.

Bubbeh's eyes widened with disapproval. "That's easy for you to say!" she scolded Jake

In Your Dreams

gently.

Jake managed to stifle his laughter.

"Of course," he said, smiling. "You're right as always, Bubbeh."

Afterword

Like the other books in The Decryptors Science Fiction Series, *In Your Dreams* contains some facts, some theory, and a good deal of imaginative fiction. It also draws on myths and legends.

As Jake's grandmother says, the Constable is similar to a golem. The story of the creation of an artificial man—or golem—is often retold in Jewish legends. In some of these legends, a golem is created to defend the Jewish people from danger. In many stories, the golem creates more problems and must be destroyed.

In the twentieth century, the golem has become a symbol of technology gone out of control. Norbert Wiener, one of the founders of information theory, wrote a book called *God & Golem, Inc.* (M.I.T. Press, 1966). Wiener was worried that human beings would eventually put too much trust in intelligent machines. He

In Your Dreams

felt that this would be particularly dangerous in matters of warfare. Wiener considered machines to be much too literal-minded for such work.

To find out more about the golem legends, read *The Golem: The Story of a Legend,* as told by Elie Wiesel (Summit Books, 1983), and *The Golem,* by Isaac Bashevis Singer (Farrar, Straus and Giroux, 1982). Another good source of golem stories and images in dance, theater, film, and visual art is *Golem! Danger, Deliverance and Art* edited by Emily D. Bilski (The Jewish Museum, New York, 1988).

According to sleep researchers, we all dream, even if we don't remember doing so. Scientists have discovered that most dreaming takes place in a state called Rapid Eye Movement (REM) sleep. During REM sleep, the sleeper's closed eyes dart rapidly. At that time, breathing and brain-wave patterns are a lot like those in the waking state.

If you wake up directly from the REM sleep stage, you can remember a dream. But even then, you may forget it again as soon as you're completely awake. Keeping a dream journal can usually improve your memory of dreams.

Other questions about dreams are a mat-

Afterword

ter of controversy. What are dreams? Why do we have them? There have been many different theories throughout human history. Those that Sibyl mentions to Jake are discussed in Fred Alan Wolf's *The Dreaming Universe* (Simon & Schuster, 1994), along with many other fascinating ideas.

Many people who have problems with nightmares learn how to wake themselves up. Jake's trick of identifying himself is one way to do it. Other people learn to continue with the dream and bring it under control. That's called *lucid dreaming,* and it can work with pleasant dreams as well as with nightmares.

In our story, Rachel mentions some ways to bring on lucid dreams. All these techniques are described in *Lucid Dreaming,* by Stephen LaBerge (Tarcher, 1985). The word *oneironaut,* meaning "explorer of the inner world of dreams," was coined by LaBerge and his colleagues at Stanford University. Much of my information on dreams and lucid dreams comes from his excellent book.

The lucid dream methods described in *Lucid Dreaming* have worked for many people. However, it usually takes much longer to learn to dream lucidly than it does for Jake and Robert in our story.

Obviously, Jake is dealing with something

more than merely dreaming. He actually enters another reality. That's where my story moves into the realm of fantasy.

The idea of parallel universes is discussed by physicist and science writer Fred Alan Wolf in *Parallel Universes* (Simon & Schuster, 1988) and *Taking the Quantum Leap* (Harper and Row, 1981). In *Space-Time and Beyond* (E.P. Dutton, Inc., 1982), Wolf and cartoonist Bob Toben take a playful look at parallel universes and many other theories based on quantum physics. Some interpretations of quantum physics predict the existence of parallel universes. In *The Dreaming Universe,* Wolf suggests that lucid dreams might give us a look at such "realities."

However, physicists don't believe that we'll be able to travel from one parallel universe to another. That's an idea that just turns up in science fiction.

Jake and Robert, like all of the Decryptors, have more adventures in store for them. Maybe someday they'll find their way back into the parallel world of this story—or into a different one altogether.

—D. F. Rider